Lockhart Mansion

By D.H. Dhaenens

Flammable Penguins Publishing

First published in Great Britain in 2022
by FLAMMABLE PENGUINS PUBLISHING

ISBN 978-0-9956967-5-4

FLAMMABLE PENGUINS PUBLISHING
International House
24 Holborn Viaduct
CITY OF LONDON
London EC1A 2BN

www.flammablepenguins.com

For Claire, who shares my mud.

To all the "mean lolitas" into whose TikToks I've stumbled

To MC Melody Doll, please send me a Melty Yen necklace

Chapter 1 - Egg

Every neighbourhood had a house like this. A dark, creaky, freaky house. This one stood on a hill overlooking the suburbs below. From a young age, they were told not to go near it. Halloween, however, meant the rules didn't count. Right?

The lights from the town felt far away now, with only the full moon lighting up the old house. This strange compact square house had been here for as long as anyone in the town could remember. Never lit up. Never decorated. Never inhabited. A stark contrast with the nearby town with its modern houses and plentiful lighting, which Jack missed right now.

"Come on, Jack. I dare you to knock!"

Jack balled his fists, legs on either side of his bicycle. You know what? Yeah. He could do it. He peeked around the teens circling him. Two others had joined him in trick and treating, and they'd been very successful. Jack's own Elliot costume, complete with E.T. in the front basket, had been a hit, and it meant he didn't have to walk. He still couldn't believe how many of his friends had preferred staying at home, probably so Monday they could brag about imaginary parties they had attended. Out of town, of course. The bravest would probably try the pub only to be thrown out on their asses by the landlord. College was bad enough with all the extra work and the threat of A-levels looming over. No, Jack had just wanted a fun night with his mates. It would probably be their last one. Next year was their final year of college, and they'd be too busy to make costumes. He suddenly realised they were all still looking at him. They'd been for real.

"Right. Watch E.T. for me," he said airily as he kicked the kickstand and got off his bike.

With a more nonchalant gesture than he felt, he pushed some of his curly hair out of his face. He could hear some nervous chuckling and whispering behind him as he walked the five steps up to the massive front door. They had better not take off without him. He'd spent hours making that E.T. dummy. The whole costume had started as a joke, but he ended up taking it much too seriously.

Something that appeared to happen to him all too often, it seemed. He glanced up at the imposing doorway, wondering if he should call the whole thing off or yell "boo" at his friends loudly and run off while they chased him. His hand reached out for the knocker, and he could feel the chilly air now that he'd taken his hands out of his parka's pockets. It was cold, and it was getting darker by the minute. The handed-out candy would soon diminish to nothing save for Sweetie Violets and Werther's. Before him, the door remained unmoving. Frozen.

"Hurry up, you helmet!" Nicolas called out at him, and he sighed.

Nicolas was the oldest, and he had vetoed his plan to try and go to the pub. Honestly, beyond Taynor, none of them were tall enough to pass for 18-year-olds. Reluctantly, Nicolas had donned his Naruto cosplay and joined them.

"Fine! I'll knock, but then we—" Turning around, he saw his friends were not looking at him. They were looking up and over his head. Faces paling in fear.

"You guys having a laugh?" His voice pitched up, and he took a few steps towards them, feet thudding down the stairs again. Whatever it was, he could not see it from the doorstep.

Clearly, it had spooked his friends, but he couldn't see it. All he noticed was that the upstairs curtain was moving softly. He shivered.

"Are you... smelling fries?" Nicolas asked, looking around in doubt.

Jack took in a deep breath. "No, I'm... I'm smelling fries."

Taynor let out a breath he'd been holding and made them all jump. Jack could see Tay shiver, even inside the inflatable dinosaur costume.

"Jeeze!" Nicolas sighed. "We should probably—"
"Nooo. You still need to knock, Jack. What are you, chicken?"

Jack made a face at his friend. It looked like he'd almost gotten away with not knocking, but now that was back on the table. A gust of wind blew some dried leaves around his ankles. This house had no pumpkins or decorations. So perhaps they should just leave it be.

"Fine. Give me a minute, though. You guys spooked the hell out of me."

He flashed a grin and went to check on his E.T. dummy, grabbing some of the candy he'd stashed in the basket. A full-sized Cadbury Chomp was retrieved, and he peeled it leisurely, eating it bite by bite.

The other kids grinned and followed his lead, looting their own trick-or-treat buckets before discerning parents could throw out all the unhealthy but delicious bits. Much to everyone's envy, Taynor had gotten a Twix, which he was now sharing with Nicolas. Somehow, nobody seemed to want to address that the frying smell grew stronger. Maybe the kebab shop down the road? A fish and chips shop?

Maybe, but one of those upscale ones, then. It smelled more like homemade fry-ups than a chip shop. And to be honest, it was making Jack hungry.

"Okay. Let's do this." Jack crumpled the wrapper and shoved it into his trouser pockets. His parents had taught him not to litter, and it would be fairer to keep them, so they had a more accurate count later on.

"Let's do this," he repeated and smacked his hands together, glad for the sound. "Nic, you get my bike, okay?"

"Like, if you die?"

4

"No, you absolute numpty, in case we need to run," Jack clarified. "You're not getting my bike."

"Oh!" Nicolas seemed slightly disappointed but mounted the bike, ready to slam the kickstand and go. "Ready when you are."

"Cheers." He took in a deep breath and grinned. Okay, this was probably not going to be anything. He was going to knock, and nothing was going to answer. He visualised it, like his mother would often tell him to do.

First, I am going to knock twice on that ancient wooden door. It will ring out all loud and creepy-like. Nothing is gonna happen. The smell of a fry-up isn't strange. We're going to laugh and run off and then get more candy.

He reminded himself that the lack of decorations probably meant nobody was living there. And if they were, they probably wouldn't open up for trick-or-treaters.

And with that, he wondered why he was ever even afraid of it in the first place. He shook loose some of the tension in his arms and mounted the steps again to the front door. This time, it seemed less imposing, at least.

He chuckled and turned around to his friends, though he was displeased to find the smell of frying... meat became stronger as he stepped closer.

He raised his hand.

"Boo!" shouted Nicolas before laughing. Jack couldn't help himself; he laughed as well and turned around with his hands up as if he was impersonating a monster. He barely remembered the commotion around the window anymore—probably for the best.

This time, however, Taynor shrieked. He started to run, while Nicolas just looked confused.

The smell of fried chicken was overpowering now. Against Jack's best instincts, he turned around.

The door was open, more than ajar.

The first thing he noticed was the smell of rot, dark and damp. And then, standing before him in the doorway was a skeletal being, covered in grey cloth faded to the same hue as its decaying skin. It seemed to have no face, the nostrils elongated and the rest of its face covered in strips of fabric as if it was bandaged. Its... hair seemed to be either made up of wispy spiderwebs or to just be the most silver thinning hair he'd ever seen. But what surprised him most was what the being, that foul being, was holding that was so contrary to this entire thing.

It was a plate of fried chicken. Not just any. The homemade kind on a dainty porcelain plate. Golden brown with flecks of freshly ground pepper. Jack couldn't help but feel the being was offering the chicken out to him, but he also didn't want to stay long enough to give a food review.

Grabbing the plate, he whipped around to scramble down the stairs in a panicked run. The sound of bones cracking. It would stay with Jack forever. The being made noise that could perhaps be speech, but he couldn't understand it. It was too soft, too cursed. He could see the thing retreating as he reached the bike and straddled the baggage carrier. He held onto the plate securely, unwilling to give up this prize for some reason. Perhaps it was just because he was hungry.

"Go go go go!" he cried out, and Nicolas did not falter. The boy kicked the kickstand and then smashed the pedals. They barrelled down the road, back towards the centre of town. The cold was now long forgotten as his jacket flapped open, E.T. almost flying off with the speed they were going.

And that was how a group of trick-or-treaters was found, running and cycling screaming, but with arguably some of the best fried chicken any of them had ever tasted in their short pimply lives.

Chapter 2 - Beginnings

The house stood empty for a while longer as if it was trying to find its bearings. The locals ignored it after the Halloween Weirdness, as the incident was now called. Though none of them could deny that the boys had come home with a plate of chicken. The porcelain plate itself had not come from any of the parents. Their *darling* sons would never dare to visit the chip shops as they had been told not to ruin their appetites with that stuff. That being said, chip shops didn't routinely offer takeaways on fine patterned china.

Luckily the house was far enough out of the way that it was easy to ignore and thus forget. The houses in the suburb rose in value to the point where the owner of the house saw some merit in trying to rent it out again. News of the renovation did spark some interest in the neighbourhood, passed along in whispers. It had to be said many were interested in whether the work would unearth any new or frightening ghosts that fried chicken and served it on dainty plates.

Ms Merril looked around as she reached the house. As the most outgoing of the parents in the town, she had volunteered to come up. There was some unfinished business they had with the house.

"Hello?" She clutched the plate under her armpit. To be honest, she was glad to return the thing and to find out whether or not it had really come from here. She would be the talk of the town. The hippie parent who had come up to the house to appease the spirits. Bullshit, of course. Though she didn't want this old-fashioned plate in her home, the real reason for her to be here was that she wished to gossip about the new inhabitants.

Mary, the estate agent, had loose lips and had let slip that it was a bunch of university-age girls, which many homeowners thought was a damn shame. They'd all hoped for a lovely family, but the house wasn't too far from the university, and the rent was very doable when split. In fact, with how long it had been on the market, Ms Merril was sure that the rent had dropped.

Mary poked her head out of the kitchen, startling Ms Merril and causing her to almost drop the Halloween plate.

"Mary! You spooked me."

"Aaah, that's the house that does that to ya." Mary's speech was a delightful informal mix when there was nobody around. "What brings you here, Lila?"

Ms Merril arranged her hair band and then grabbed the plate from under her armpit. "The... um... plate."

Mary looked quizzically at the empty dish before remembering.

"Oh yes! The Halloween incident. How is Tay doing?" She took the plate and looked over it. "You know, we had the police turn the house inside out. Nothing or nobody was found."

Mary shrugged and walked to the cabinet.

"I still wonder if there was some prankster who made camp here for the night, but..." She shrugged and gingerly put the plate back. Ms Merril jealously looked around the top-of-the-line white goods and the large American fridge. Even the smaller appliances were either Smeg or John Lewis, at least. Another way to try and lure anyone to live here, she guessed, though she wouldn't consider moving up here for love or money.

The place seemed simply cursed. Whether that was because nobody lasted here very long or maybe because it had stood empty for so long now... But surely, builders would have spotted something here was amiss?

Even those small and reasonable assurances didn't help quiet the little voice in her head that worried about what her son had seen on All Hallows' Eve.

Tay wasn't one for flights of fancy, and in fact, she sometimes wished he would be a touch more whimsical. Allowing him to trick or treat at sixteen had been considered strange by her neighbour. Still, she was mostly glad to see him excited and planning costumes rather than watching those filthy gory movies or, worse, going partying with boys older than him.

"So students, huh? I guess it is that time of year." She steered the conversation airily.

"Yep. Owner has given up on families. There's simply not that much demand for four-bedroom houses anymore, and you can't lower the rent much more than it already is. So, we looked at a different target demographic. Students." Mary shrugged. "Tea, Lila? I'm going to shove some cookies in the oven, liven the place up with that smell."

"Tea sounds absolutely delightful, Mary. About that smell. Were you here after the Halloween incident?" Ms Merril asked.

"Yes, the police called me as I had a key and the owner was outta town. It was just so weird!" She ripped open a pack of store-bought cookie dough, the variety that came in cubes that you melted and baked in nice circles. Not really Ms Merril's favourite, but she admired the originality of Mary's approach.

"So weird?" Ms Merril picked up her line of questioning again as Mary had become concentrated on arranging the little squares of dough.

"Oh! Yes, it smelled like a chip shop here. The frying pan was soaking, but the next morning it was back where it always is. Like… they came back to finish the washing up."

"This ghost already sounds like more of a gentleman than my Gene," teased Ms Merril before she realised she had called it a ghost. It felt improper.

Mary let out a nervous chuckle and turned on the combination oven.

"Yes. Or the squatter didn't wanna leave fingerprints or some shit," she then rushed to the retro-looking kettle and filled it with water. Everything here smelled new. New appliances. New furniture, fresh paint even. It was hard to imagine someone had been busy cooking in this virginal kitchen and that any squatter would care enough to return to do the dishes.

She shook her head. No, a squatter would have left this place in tatters.

"So, when are your students arriving? I hope they're nice people."

"Oh yes, three girls. Very kind."

Mary swore as she trapped her finger in the oven switch briefly.

"Motherf—" She cleared her throat. "Yes, very nice," she repeated and finally managed to slam the tray down into the oven.

Chapter 3 - Ramona

"Sorry, I'm late!" Ramona jumped out of the moving van, looking around, only to see that she was not too late for a change. Nobody else had arrived yet. She ran her hands over the back of her skirt.

It made her a little sad that nobody was here to witness this victory. At the very least, nobody would give her weird looks for lighting a cigarette.

She made sure to lock the doors of the small van and glanced around briefly. The place was huge, old-fashioned. There would be some fantastic outfit shots taken here. The bushes by the corners alone were breath-taking. While the house was old, the interior had been redone. Best of both worlds, the real estate agent had sold it as.

As she lit the cigarette, she checked her phone. As usual, Valiant was on her way with a detailed ETA. George, true to form, just sent curt messages in the group chat confirming that she would be there. What else did they want, gosh?
She scoffed and put her phone away again.
It was her first time sharing a house with people who weren't her family, and it was... nerve-wracking, to say the least. George and Valiant were some of her closest friends, she'd known them

through college, and all three girls had gotten into lolita fashion in the last few years.

George had been the first. She had been making dresses since early high school. Which then became second-hand dresses from Chinese resellers, then the hit-or-miss-but-mostly-miss month where she only bought replicas until she had finally discovered her favorite brand, *Manifesteange Metamorphose Temps de Fille*. A prominent Japanese brand that was about as chaotic as Ramona's own wardrobe.

Ramona had been attracted to the fashion herself for a while, but it wasn't until finally, George sold her first mis-buys that she got her hands on any of the brand dresses she'd been admiring from afar. Ever since, Ramona had haphazardly accumulated dresses. Anything she liked and could afford, she bought. Hence the need for a moving truck. Her wardrobe alone was about six boxes.

Valiant was their latest addition. She'd really only started after college, when the uniforms could finally be left behind, and had launched herself headlong in only the most pastel and cutesy of lolita fashion offshoots: sweet lolita. Val's wardrobe was mainly *Angelic Pretty*, *Baby, the Stars Shine Bright* and some Taobao releases. Whatever fit her definition of cute made it into her wardrobe.

Ramona wiped some ashes off of her *Moi-Meme-Moitie* OP[1]. It was a chiffon miracle in all black, with a square neckline and a corset-style belt. She'd combined it with long gloves and a simple headpiece made of a strip of black lace. Perhaps not the most practical outfit to handle furniture and move boxes in, but she would have been devastated to lose this dress in the move. She kicked a pebble and stubbed out her cigarette when it was done.

Time to at least start unloading. She'd only rented the van for a few hours, and soon she would have to drive it back to town. She wondered how the other girls managed their transport as she threw open the back doors.

Valiant probably had her parents offer to drive her, which was sweet. And then George would probably endeavor to bring everything from the train station herself.

Nope, she was soon proven wrong on one of the two. A station wagon, one of those taxis you call with an app, was pulling up and parked in front of the house in the large courtyard.

Was it a courtyard? The house had a large gravel circle out front. The large garden and lawn were wrapped with fencing and fronted by an imposing iron gate. The wide meandering road was large enough to drive a small truck comfortably up to the house. The private taxi parked behind her van, and George got out,

---

[1] OP stands for one piece, a dress that covers the shoulders and can be worn without a blouse.

arranging her petticoats and walking quickly round to the boot of the station wagon.

"Hey. Need a hand?" Ramona smiled.

"It's fine. It's not that much." George's swift hands dragged three large suitcases out of the back of the car before waving the driver off absently.

"That guy deserves a solid five stars. Not a single attempt at talking."

Ramona grinned and wiped some of her curls out of her hair. "Valiant's on her way. Want to head inside?"

"Yeah." Ramona could see her friend eyeing up the steep front steps. There were only five of them, but they were high and not very suitcase-friendly.

"I'll help you up." She put her own box back into the van and took one of the suitcases. "Jeeze! What's in here?"

"You be careful with that!" George sighed. "That's only my petticoats. And hoop skirts."

"Aha." She must have stuffed that poor suitcase to the brim. "Nothing fragile then."

"You better not be implying anything." George gave her a warning look, but Ramona just rolled her eyes and dragged the suitcase up the stairs.

"Thanks," George begrudgingly said. She followed behind Ramona with her second suitcase.

The door swung open, and Ramona almost fell backward off the stairs, bumping into George.

"Fuck. It's the estate agent," she gasped and looked up. "Hi! Mary, right?"

Mary pulled a face at the abrupt cursing. She smiled, clearly placated, when George remembered her name correctly.

"Yes, come in," Mary smiled pleasantly, resuming her professional facade as she dove back into the house.

Ramona scrunched her face in mockery at George, who just shrugged and continued up into the house after the estate agent.

"Smells absolutely delightful in here," said George, glancing around.

Ramona had to agree. She had no idea why this house had been empty for so long. It was a beautiful house with modern interiors and fixings. Right down to the super-fast internet, which was fiber or at least something fancy that went really fast. It was expensive, but the bills were included. Considering the rent price, they were getting a steal, even if it had a bedroom more than they really needed. Perhaps they could discuss getting another housemate at some point.

"Ah, thank you. I just threw together some cookies for you girls!" Mary beamed, though Ramona could see her scrabble to put some packaging in the bin.

"That's really very kind, but you shouldn't have..." Ramona put the large suitcase down near the first and looked around at the open-plan kitchen.

"Sooo, you girls... are... studying... fashion?" Mary tried.

Ramona laughed, glad that George had taken off to pick up her third bag.

"Oh, oh no. I'm a biology major. George is studying linguistics, and Valiant—she's coming later—she studies art history." It was a common theme. They dressed in big skirts with lots of frills, so they had to be showgirls or fashion designers. Why else would anyone dress in something so ridiculous?

"Oh!" Mary smiled. "That's great."

She clearly wanted to say more. "Soo... you guys dressed up for the occasion?"

George was trying so hard not to roll her eyes as she returned. Ramona could tell by how the other girl turned away from the conversation.

"No... This is just what we wear. I mean. It's a hobby, but also, what we wear, and—"

"It's our clothes. Jeans are just dreadful," George piped up. "Ramona, let's get that lorry emptied out. You just know Valiant's gonna need the space to unload."

"Yeah!" Ramona sighed, relieved. "Excuse us. I've gotta get the van back into town in less than an hour."

Mary nodded, whipping around to get the cookies out of the oven.

Ramona walked down the stairs again, skirt bouncing with each step, glad she'd grabbed some simple boots for today's move.

"What do you think?"

"Of the estate lady? She's—"

"The house, George," laughed Ramona, opening the doors to the van and grabbing one of the bigger boxes. "I know you only saw it once before."

"I believe it should be quite adequate, to be honest," she said and looked over. "The house itself is quite beautifully designed. It's honestly baffling how it has remained empty for so long."

"It's a huge house," said Ramona. "Not that many families need four giant bedrooms. I mean, you've seen them. This place is like a mansion."

She was still impressed she had managed to find it for such a reasonable price. It was actually a steal! The rent between the three of them would be pretty easy to manage. If anything, the only trouble would be that it would be hard to keep clean, but she was sure they could look at a cleaner if it got too much. After all, they all had their jobs and their studies.

"I suppose." George grabbed another box and followed Ramona up the stairs to drop off the boxes. "Are you quite sure there are no hidden surprises? Like a huge council tax or some... frightful landlord who insists on living in?"

"No, the landlord's a family guy living in town. I mean, if you're curious, I asked if anyone died here, and he said no."

"That's so American of you, Ramona. Of course someone's died here at some point."

"But not violently. That's what I asked him." Ramona grinned. The houses here were so old that it was almost impossible that nobody had died in them in the hundred or so years it had been standing. Since moving from the US, Ramona had found her new country's history quite fascinating. American ghost stories always relied on people dying violently in a house, but with the average age of buildings here, if that was true, probably every place was haunted. So, it was more likely that ghosts just weren't real.

Ramona plopped the box down and skipped down the stairs again. "Thanks for your help. Shouldn't be very long now." She scrunched her nose and realized she was starting to copy George's fancier speech patterns. George had once mentioned her family believed itself to be relatively upper class, though Ramona had been too embarrassed to say she had no clue what that meant. It seemed to either have something to do with money or acting fancier, but the English class system was still a mystery to her. Luckily, as a yank, she got away with asking all the questions. "Not at all," George replied, already on her third box. Ramona was always surprised at how strong the girl was.

"Just lucky the place is furnished, eh?"

"Quite. I would rather not set up a washing machine on the first day in a new house," George replied. "There is quite enough to do without all that nonsense."

"It's not too bad. At least bills are included, so we just have to do some basics before we settle in too much."

She grinned and looked around. It really was a stunning area. The relative distance meant they had a lot of quiet, and the landlord had given them permission for the odd party, given they let him know in advance.

The sound of gravel being crunched made her look up. "Ah— That's..."

Ramona's eyes went wide as a brand new hybrid arrived out front. "What the—"

Valiant grinned and hopped out of the car. "Look, guys! My parents got me a car! This is going to be so handy for us!" Valiant squeed, almost losing the flower crown perched on her head as she jumped in place.

Ramona raised an eyebrow, but her friend was not wrong. They would need to do groceries, and the delivery radius did not reach here, even from the town. One pizzeria delivered here, but that was about it.

"That's wonderful, Valiant. Congratulations," said George. A larger old-fashioned car looking as expensive as the new hybrid stopped behind Valiant, with her parents getting out.

Ramona turned away and started to get the last few boxes. The front yard was getting quite busy with all these cars, and she wanted to get this over with. Families made her uncomfortable.

Her parents had moved here with her, but Ramona was on her own beyond that. They certainly weren't buying her cars or helping her move into housing, even if she got a small allowance. They were more of a... distant family, seeing each other on holidays and keeping communication minimal, and she liked it that way. Now nineteen and quite capable, she didn't need help from her family unless some horrible emergency came up. So, Valiant's bouncy family and their affection struck her as odd.

"Congrats." Ramona grinned. "I better get all of this in. I need to get the van back."

"Sure! We'll park out of the way!" Valiant promised, getting into her brand new car again to move it into one of the parking spots as her parents started unloading her belongings. Of course, these were in nice plastic boxes and new-looking suitcases, not the re-used moving boxes George and Ramona were using.

If George was perturbed, as she would say, by the show of family affection, she didn't show it. Before grabbing two small boxes and bringing them into the house, she nabbed one of the cookies from the kitchen counter.

"Alright, I'm almost done," said Ramona, heading over to grab the last two boxes. Valiant was starting to head over with her first box as she did. This was going to be a long day.

At last, the van was empty, and she sat her butt behind the wheel to drive it back into town. There was going to be some unpacking—it seemed she had brought more stuff than the other two girls, but to be fair, there were many things she owned that she wouldn't need in this house she didn't want to let go of. Her electric kettle had been an investment; even if this house came with one, she didn't want to just throw it out. It could just stay in the box. Be a backup or be ready for her to use in another house if she had to move out. This was the first time she was sharing with others, and her family had considered the idea rather strange, but they'd let her be when they heard how much less in rent she would need to pay at the new address.

Still, she had some sort of feeling the house was wrong somehow. Too good to be true and all that, no?

The landlord had assured her the house was fine. Newly renovated. There had been an incident with a probable squatter last Halloween, but the house had been turned around and refitted with new locks to make sure nobody could get in. She hadn't shared that with the other girls, but it wouldn't really make a difference, would it? Some guy had seen an empty house and taken the opportunity. That was all. She sighed. There was probably a lot of crime in towns like this one, but she knew they would be fine as long as they locked their doors. They weren't that far away from town.

She turned the van onto the main road, passing the family scene, and cleared her mind to focus on the drive.

Chapter 4 – Ramona

The smell of pizza filled the lounge as they chatted in the dimly lit lounge. It was somewhat cold; the girls hadn't *quite* figured out the heating yet, but nobody was complaining. Blankets and hoodies simply added to the adventurous atmosphere. The first night in their own place! It was a delightful thought still. A few boxes, mostly Ramona's, were still scattered around, but she promised she would get to them soon.

"I can't wait to get groceries tomorrow. I mean, look at that kitchen," Valiant sighed at the sight of the open-plan kitchen not too far away from where they were sitting. Lit up by the cute spotlights, it looked pretty clean and friendly.

Ramona nodded. "I hope they sell Kraft Mac & Cheese."

"Ramona! We'll finally be able to cook with more than a microwave, a kettle, and a dodgy blender, and you're thinking of mac and cheese?" laughed Valiant.

"It's easy!" Ramona whined back defensively.

George intervened, "Well, you should be able to meal prep with the size of that fridge."

"Yes," Valiant acquiesced. "That's my plan, at least. We can get a bunch of vegetables, and I cannot wait to do tray bakes, honestly."

"Your brownies are pretty good." Ramona grabbed the last slice of her pizza and sighed. "Think there's a lolita community down here? We can host meets!"

"I don't know about that," Valiant said. "The estate agent said the house isn't very popular with the locals."

Ramona frowned. "You know I spoke with the owner once. He says there's nothing actually wrong with the house."

She wondered briefly if she should tell the Halloween story but decided against it. It was late, and Valiant might get frightened. She had never lived in some inner city as she had, and even George was quite fancy. It wouldn't surprise Ramona if George's parents' house was as big as this.

"Maybe it's just too enormous to rent out," said George. "It could easily be subdivided, though."

"But why put in the money when you can't rent it out as is? And perhaps this is one of those protected buildings," said Valiant, shrugging. "Face it. It's probably haunted."

At that moment, one of the boxes slid to the floor with a loud thump. Ramona jumped.

"Jeeze!" She got up and went to check. "I guess we didn't stack these right."

"You should just take them up to your room." George wiped her hands. "I can help."

"That'd be good." Ramona had stopped moving boxes up when the time came to order some food before the pizzeria closed, but really she wanted these things out of the way. Between the three of them, she was aware she was the most scatterbrained, and it would take real effort not to annoy her housemates.

Valiant chuckled. "I'll clean up here. Anyone wanna keep the leftover pizza?"

"Hell, yes." Ramona could not imagine throwing it out.

"Positively, yes," George added, looking toward Ramona with a chuckle.

Ramona picked up the other box. "Let's get this bread," she said, starting up the stairs as George just gave her a weird look.

"Ah, don't worry about it," said Ramona. "So, once these three boxes are up in my room, we've officially moved in."

"Well, there's still the internet coming tomorrow, and we must have the boiler and electricity checked, but I suppose you are right."

Ramona opened the door to her room with a shove of her hips and almost dropped the box. One of them had been opened and rifled through. A blouse was thrown halfway across the room, and several other items were hanging unfurled over the edges. No longer the neat tight rolls she had packed them as, now, all spilled out on the floor in loose piles.

"What—" She looked around the box on its side. All the windows were closed, and nothing else seemed amiss.

She raised a hand to her mouth. "What the hell!" She rushed over and started looking at her belongings.

"Are they okay? What was in there?"

"Mostly blouses and skirts." She took a deep breath. "Nothing's been ripped or broken, though." She sat back, relieved.

"Who could have done this? The window looks locked. Nobody could have entered while we were downstairs..." George quickly put the box down and checked the window.

"Were you up here—"

George raised an eyebrow. "Did I go rifling through your clothes to pinch a few brand blouses? Oh, naturally. That is how I acquire all my brand items, you see: rifling through housemates' belongings." She crossed her arms and walked out of the room.

Ramona closed her eyes. Of course, it hadn't been George. She'd seen her friend most of the evening while they were busying themselves downstairs.

"George, I'm sorry!" she called after her.

Oh, for fuck's sake, why had she said that? She took a deep breath and walked back down the stairs.

"George. I am sorry. I should have known better."

"Water under the bridge, as one says." George smiled a little. "Come on. Let's get your stuff upstairs. There isn't any food in these, right?"

"You're thinking rats?" Ramona frowned.

"We have rats?" Valiant cried out from the kitchen. "Eeeewww."

"Calm down, Valiant. Most older houses have mice or small vermin. We're just brainstorming as one of Ramona's boxes was pushed over."

"What about a cat?" Valiant squeaked. "I may have…"

"A cat?" George grinned suddenly. "Don't tell me you brought Socks! Actually, please do!"

"Yes." Valiant walked out and returned with the small tuxedo cat in her arms. "I'm sorry I didn't tell you guys. My parents only agreed to let me take him today, and… well… The contract did say pets allowed."

"This is amazing!" George grinned. "Oh, who's the best little bandit? Did you go ransacking the clothes?"

Ramona sighed. "I wish you'd told us sooner, but I'm quite happy to have a cat as long as you do all the annoying stuff."

"Of course. It's my cat." Valiant put the cat down and smiled a little. "Thanks, you guys. He'll be an indoor kitty for now. After a few months, we'll see."

"There's a great garden he can... go in," Ramona said.

"Sweetie, cats use litter boxes. It's fine." Valiant blinked. "I've set a few up near the back door and one near the storage closet. That should be plenty."

"Ah, lovely." George stopped cooing over the feline. "Alright. Any more surprises we should process tonight?"

"No." Ramona shrugged. "I'll just get my last box upstairs, and then I'm done!" The atmosphere had taken quite a positive turn. Valiant tended to have that effect on people. She was just naturally kind and inviting, though she was shy sometimes. Perhaps that was why she had brought her cat and had not really told any of them.

Having a furry friend there was heart-warming, even if it weighed only ten pounds and presented a mortal danger to chiffon.

Chapter 5 - Ramona

The rest of the evening had gone quite chill. The gang set up an impossibly large cat tree for Socks and had decided to relax with a movie.

By now, the only thing to illuminate the large lounge was the TV and a single kitchen light left on so Socks could find his food and water bowls.

Ramona found herself missing large parts of the old movie as she dozed off. It was some kind of silly comedy that she'd seen before, but she hadn't wanted to drag out their choice any further than necessary. There was a creak, and she briefly wondered if Socks was getting into trouble. Stretching out, she slipped off of the sofa. Valiant was watching intently; George looked like she had lost interest and was just checking her phone. Very likely a gossip chat.

"Guys. Do you believe in ghosts?" she suddenly asked. There was something about this house. How had a tiny dumb cat managed to sneak into her room when the door was closed? The more she thought about it, the less likely it seemed that Socks was what had caused the chaos in her room.

Valiant paused the movie and frowned. The light from the TV made her blonde and pink hair look kind of purple.

"Seriously? Ghosts?" She shook her head. "No. It would make historians' lives much easier if they did exist. But they don't," she said and looked over to George.

George shrugged, barely looking up from her phone.

"I would not know, to be honest," she said carefully. "Apparitions, sure. But actual ghosts?" She shook her head.

"There is much to be said for the scientific reasonings behind—"

Suddenly, there was a loud bang upstairs. Socks rushed by and hid under the love seat couch, his meow affirming and lodging his innocence for all to hear.

"That was not—" Ramona lifted her head up and looked at the ceiling. "Let's go."

"Why?" cried George. "I would say no. I cannot abide by this nonsense."

"What if it's in your room? You didn't pack everything away in your closet yet, did you?" Valiant went white.

George stood up and reached into her backpack for her hand-cranked torch.

"We are going," she decided, looking a bit silly as she cranked the device in her hands.

Still, Ramona got up. She didn't want to turn off the TV as it at least provided them with some light.

"Do you think it's a burglar?"

"Nah, probably a ghost that heard you talk shit," Ramona replied to Valiant, who snorted. George took the lead and marched straight toward the steps, flipping on lights wherever she passed them by. A good decision, but Ramona just wished she'd grabbed her phone from the charger. This stuff was seriously scary, and the shadows flickering in the small beam of the windup torch did not help. She sighed and hoped that George was as brave as she looked. Then again, if her brand was threatened, there was no telling what she'd do.

George stomped up the stairs, sure to scare away anything smaller than Socks. Socks had not joined their little expedition, probably for the best. They didn't need to be spooked by the cat at the worst possible time. The stairway came up in the middle of the second floor, with the four rooms in the corners. In the north, between the two bedrooms, and toward the west, two bathrooms were perched between the rooms. The girls had claimed the three roomiest rooms, while the smallest one would be fought over for storage later. They stayed together, walking in silence as George opened up her door. Nothing. Everything seemed to have remained undisturbed.

As she turned around to shine the light over the furniture, Valiant flicked the light on with little decorum.

Nothing. The room was empty, and considering they had only just moved in, Ramona was surprised at how tidy it was. Stacked against the wall, the cardboard boxes made a neat pile, and the bed was already made, no doubt a priority after such a long day. With some shame, Ramona had to admit, if only to herself, she would have to sort out her bedding before laying her head down for the night. Remembering George's room also had access to an ensuite bathroom, Ramona walked the short distance to the room, hesitated a moment, then flicked on the light. Ramona could hear her own sigh of relief echoing in the silence.

"So, it was clearly not in this room. Let's go have a gander at your rooms." George turned around and turned off the light in her room, though Valiant had switched on the hallway light this time. With the darkness outside, the light made the whole place look... gloomy. It was clear now, but the artificial light did very little against the oppressive darkness looming outside on the house grounds. The town lights were dim and distant. A spooky atmosphere that reminded her of cold winter mornings— wrapped up warm, walking in the early morning fog on her way to school. Unable to see beyond a few steps.

Valiant took the lead as they headed to her room and threw the door open. Nothing. Nothing scuttled or slithered.
"Your room next."
Valiant looked through her room briefly, but there was nothing amiss unless her army of stuffed toys had taken to an uprising. Again, Valiant took the lead as they headed for the last of their three rooms. George rushed to the side of Valiant and flipped open her door, in one movement reaching for the light switch, flooding the room with light and...

Nothing. There was a mannequin, an old dress resting loosely on it, the zipper removed. Next to the improperly attired dressmaker's doll, sheets lay dropped on the floor. Ramona had grabbed them to make the bed but had gotten distracted when the pizza came. Leaving them forgotten on the floor.

"New project already?" Valiant asked.

"It was twenty-five quid on Lace Market[2]. You don't get to judge me." Ramona glared.

"Don't you have that exact same dress in—" Valiant was shushed with a finger to her lips.

"What was that, missy *I-need-to-organize-three-shopping-services-to-get-all-colourways*?" Ramona rebutted.

Valiant's lips tensed.

Ramona grinned for a second and removed her finger. Perhaps there had been nothing wrong at all, and they were all just panicking over a branch of a nearby tree hitting the roof. But George was looking away from her room, and Ramona didn't like where her eyes were going.

"The fourth bedroom?" Valiant broke the silence.

"Yeah. We should check it just in case." George sounded braver than Ramona felt, but at the same time, that wasn't hard. She would've given everything to just drop this whole thing and go to bed, pretending they weren't in a giant house with strange noises. Perhaps they were just imagining things. Perhaps.

George had already taken three long steps toward the furthest room. It was the furthest away from the stairs and bathroom, so it hadn't been that popular when it came to doling out rooms.

Ramona rolled her eyes and walked along, her stockinged feet now feeling the cold even through the carpeted floor. This side of the house definitely didn't get as much sun.

---

[2] Lace Market is a popular website for the sale of second-hand lolita garments between lolitas. Kind of like eBay but with more salt.

Valiant took her turn in opening the door, flicking the switch. Light flooded the room, but again—anticlimactically—nothing. The room was relatively small, with the rafters looming over the entire space. Very dramatic, very goth. Very freaking cold.

Ramona turned away. "All happy now? I'm just going to go to bed, I think."

Valiant nodded. "Does anyone mind if I bring Socks upstairs?" She had her worried face on.

"Of course not, Valiant. I hear cats are excellent at detecting ghosts."

Carefully, George turned off the light and closed the door.

"Not this one. He'd sleep right through it, but I'd rather keep my eye on him in a new house."

"That's fair," Ramona agreed with a shrug. While she was more of a dog person, just the same, the thought of a scared cat roaming the downstairs area made her heart ache. Even though it probably would result in a lot of yelling and scratching rather than actual sadness. Either way, she was happy to oblige.

And hopefully, the rest of the night would go well. Not exactly the kind of Friday night she had expected when starting university, but she would take what she could get.

As Valiant walked down to pick up her cat and turn off all the lights, Ramona walked to her room and collapsed onto the bed. Nope, she had to make the damn thing first. With a groan, she sat back up and walked over to the pile of sheets. Being an adult sucked. As they all seemed to get ready for bed, she could hear metal music blaring from Valiant's room and George's not-so-quiet scuffling, no doubt unpacking all her belongings efficiently and neatly, as one should. Or at least, as George would say, and Ramona probably should.

Ramona laughed a bit at her self-chastisement before throwing the sheet into the air and letting it land over the bed.

This couldn't all just be a coincidence. Clothes having been... rifled through, for lack of a better phrase. The banging. Part of her wanted to believe it was all just a silly coincidence, but at the same time, what if there was something here?

No, just nerves about the move. Since moving to the United Kingdom, it was the first time that she was living in a house again. Until now, at least in England, her other dwellings had been small flats, with their own noises, mostly from neglect and neighbors. Not to mention that one winter, she got bronchitis because the landlord, Mr. All-Bills-Included, had locked the thermostat behind a plastic cage so nobody could touch it.

This place was heaven compared. It would only be for a year, maybe two, while they worked on their degrees, and only for as long as they all got on. They hadn't done too badly as friends, and their shared interest in lolita fashion had helped a lot with that. Their styles were different. Valiant's style was the most diverse, with her pastels, plushies, and random metal bands. Then there was George, mild-mannered, quiet George, softly spoken but always ready to stand up for her friends or herself. Something they had often needed when hanging out, and people started to harass them.

And then there was her. Nothing exceptional. She was the yank who had moved to the UK and had only just begun to find friends through her love for lolita fashion. It had saved her from so much loneliness. She loved the lolita community she had gotten to know around her area. The sheer fact that two of her friends from the comm had become so close they could share a house together warmed her heart.

With a shake of her head, she focused on the task at hand— making the bed. She pulled the elasticated sheet tightly over the mattress, glad she'd picked the correct size. Then it was time for the duvet and her pillow, her least favorite part. She always took ages getting it right. With a sigh, she started looking for corners.

"Would you like some assistance?" George was standing in the doorway with her pajamas on a vintage-looking set with ruffles and a cute floral pattern.

"Yes, please," Ramona sighed, hands still scouring the duvet to find the corners. George grabbed the duvet corner and expertly turned it inside out, taking over the corners from Ramona when she had finally found them. George took only a few shakes to get the blanket completely sorted. Ramona stared in disbelief before grabbing the pillow and unceremoniously stuffing it into the pillowcase.

"Thank you."

"Not to worry. I've done this kind of thing quite a lot," beamed George, shaking the duvet out over the bed. George's hands hovered over the sides for a bit, as if she was contemplating making the bed proper, but then she turned around. Luckily. Ramona didn't think she could live down having her friend, who was not to put too fine a point on it one year younger, make the bed for her.

"I don't think it was the cat that got at your clothes," she said suddenly, gaze fixed on the box of clothes on the floor.

"Yeah, me neither. But what else could it have been?" sighed Ramona, sitting down.

George sat down on the bed as well.

"Well, when I told a friend I was moving here, he told me... stories of the place." She cleared her throat. "Ghost stories about the big scary mansion on the outskirts of town."

"Sounds kind of like this house." Ramona frowned.

"Quite. It is this house," said George, glancing around. "There's something... off about it, don't you think? This house should have sold long ago, especially with all the work put into it."

"That's true. This isn't exactly a grotty flat under a subway overpass. Tube... tube, I mean."

She caught her own American turn of phrase, but if George noticed it, she said nothing, merely running her hands through her long honey-brown hair.

"Unfortunately, I am not one to believe in ghosts."

She let her hair hang in front of her right shoulder. "But most importantly, you were not surprised to hear about this place having ghastly rumors about it going around."

"No..." Ramona sighed. "Ya got me. I heard something as well." She threw her hands up.

"Aha." George looked over and then nodded. "That makes a lot more sense. You spoke to the landlord, did you not?"

"I did indeed. I heard some… interesting anecdotes."

She swallowed. "We probably shouldn't keep it from Valiant, though. Let's get her into this conversation." It didn't seem right to hide this kind of thing from their housemate, even if she was most likely to be a scaredy cat about it.

"Right you are," said George, getting up to bang on Valiant's door. "Valiant! Turn that noise down!" she called. Her first few bangs on the door were lost in a pretty enthusiastic drum solo.

Finally, the loud metal music stopped, and Valiant opened the door, dressed in a long pink nightgown with adorable bears and cats on it, her hair half in rollers.

"What is it?" she asked.

"We must talk about the house. Bring your rollers. My room," George asserted.

"I like it here," Valiant sighed, grabbing her basket with the warm rollers to join her two friends.

"That's not it, Valiant. We're not moving away or anything dumb like that," George said, opening the door to her room for them.

"Alright then, what is it?" As she walked, Valiant was twisting her hair around one of the curlers.

"Well, we gotta come clean about this place," said Ramona. "I've heard stories. George heard stories. So, we wanted to make sure everyone was at the same level, get it?"

"No secrets, after all. Or not too many." George winked and grabbed a few pillows from her bed, sitting on one so her friends could take the bed. Typical of her.

"So?" Valiant asked, sitting down on the bed and looking at the both of them.

"Sooo..." Ramona looked to George to see if she wanted to start.

George sighed. "The house has the reputation of being haunted," she said, bluntly as ever. If Valiant was surprised, she didn't show it, merely nodding as if that was what she had expected to hear. She straightened her sleeves to cover her hands more.

"Well, don't stop there. Haunted how?" she asked.

"Some of the residents in town had stories—stories of something lurking behind the windows and stalking around at night. Apparitions, such things. The story goes that there was a young man in town, Adam Lockhart, who built this house for his eventual family, but he was drafted into the second World War before it was properly finished. It is said he died in the war and that his spirit returned home, but that the ghost is confused because the premises differ from when he left," she explained, trying to keep from smiling.

"Utterly ridiculous, of course, but it's a sweet kind of story. The house is about the right age for the story to make sense, even if the architecture is a little bit old-fashioned. But the ghost of a fallen soldier has a certain... air of romance, does it not?" George grinned. "Searching for a place to rest his weary head, finding himself trapped between the familiar and the new, and here we are to disturb even more of poor Adam Lockhart's rest by moving things around."

The silence hung for a moment before Ramona chortled. "That's quite different from the story I heard, I gotta admit," she said, shaking her head. "I heard the whole, 'oh, it's all haunted' thing, but..." She looked over and shrugged.

39

"So, what's the story you heard then?" Valiant turned to her, a glint in her eyes. Far from being scared, she seemed to be enjoying this! Perhaps they all treated her much more delicately than needed.

"Well…" laughed Ramona. "Before we moved, I had the week off, so I came to explore the town. You know, look around, see what the nightlife is like. Spoiler alert, this town really just has none, but, you know… We're not the biggest party animals, to begin with."

Valiant chuckled at that. "Yeah, we'll probably be too busy trying not to fail our courses. I will, at least. You guys are much—"

"Shush," George said. "Don't talk down on yourself. You just really need to work on it, and you're going to make it just fine."

She smiled and sat back on her pillow. "We are all graduating together. Promise you that. Ghosts or not."

"Yes! Ghost stories!" she said, turning to Ramona. "Come on, your turn. Though that one's a hard one to follow up."

"Agreed," said Ramona, inclining her head. "So, as I was saying, I was here a few days before we moved," she explained. "I met the owner of the place! They got a great deal on this about ten years ago, after the last people moved out, complaining of, well… weird noises. Stuff being moved. Ghost-like stuff, but… you know, they didn't believe in that stuff, so they just thought the house was defective and sold it. Either way, the house got this whole big makeover, and nobody ever heard or saw a thing while remodeling. But it didn't sell, either, until we all moved in, so it stood empty for a while. And last Halloween, some kids came up here on a dare. One dared the other to knock and all of that, and they messed around for a bit... Finally, the one kid knocked, and... the door was opened."

Valiant gasped. "No way! The ghost?"

"This is where it gets weird. The kids say they saw... something like a ghost, but it looked seven foot tall, grotesque. Covered in blood and cobwebs, its voice booming. In exchange for their souls, it offered them a plate of fried chicken. Cursed fried chicken!"

George started laughing. "Surely, that must have been some sort of joke!"

"That's the thing; that's what everyone thinks! The kids rushed back into town with the big plate of chicken, and it was apparently really good chicken as well."

George shrugged. "Whether it was true or not, the plate they had matched one from the house, so unless the kids snuck in and made themselves fried chicken before running off with it..."

"No way, surely," George said. "What did the owner think?"

"Well, he thinks it was a squatter. But why would a squatter make trick-or-treaters fried chicken? That's what I'm struggling with, you know," pondered Ramona, taking a deep breath. "Apparently, after they ran, the house did smell like fried oil, but nothing was out of place."

"So, either a squatter made some trick-and-treaters fried chicken, washed up everything and replaced it, or it was the ghost of a fast-food worker because I don't think Adam's ghost would have even known how to make fried chicken. A young man of that age, they wouldn't have known how to cook." Ramona shrugged. "It's a weird story, but this is a weird house."

Valiant giggled. "Wow. I'm not sure what's up with this house, but I hope it's the ghost. For now, it's the most likely cause of all this trouble." She shook her head.

"Bed time, though. A lot of unpacking to do tomorrow, and I want to be able to make some home-cooked food tomorrow night, or we'll have to order pizza again."

By this stage of the evening, George's hair was entirely up in rollers, and Ramona smiled at the very old-fashioned look that gave the young girl. *How did she even sleep in those?* she wondered. *With a bit of net around the curlers, perhaps?*

"Yes, agreed," George got up and picked up her pillow.

Ramona nodded. "Yeah. Goodnight, girls. I'll see you tomorrow."

"Not too early, please."

George stood up and stretched out. "I'm quite knackered, to be honest."

Ramona nodded and sorted her bed out, looking around briefly.

"Will Socks be okay?"

"Oh yeah," Valiant said. "He's probably asleep on my bed already, anyway. He's not very adventurous, but I'm just happy to have him in the house." She smiled and walked to the door.

Ramona nodded. Her own car and her own pet. She was making herself very comfortable, very fast, and it made her worry a bit, to be honest. It wasn't her house; it was theirs. Luckily, the fact the place came furnished helped with a lot of that—when you moved in together, there was always at least one person with the most stuff that seemed to take over the place.

Valiant seemed to be that person—somehow, without even needing furniture to fill out the space.

She saw the two other girls off to their rooms, then slipped into her own bed, turning off the lights and looking toward the window. The cool cotton sheets were just starting to warm up, but she was comfortable. They would soon need the heating on, however.

What was it about this place? So far, everything could be explained away if you got a little creative. A squatter with a sense of humor. A cat getting stuck in a cardboard box and flailing to get out until the box fell over. The noises of a slightly older house, having lain empty for so long, settling and shifting. Wood creaks, heat expanding, all of that scientific stuff.

Yet, a part of her was excited. What if there was a ghost? Would she see it? Or would she not be sensitive enough to even notice when it was around them? Her brain raced, longer and longer, until it finally lured her to the land of sleep.

Chapter 6 – Ramona

Ramona woke up early in the morning, rolling around the bed. This bed was much larger than the one she'd had in her tiny flat last year, so it felt like heaven to just have space to sprawl and stretch out. And, most of all, to have a day off to do so. She was used to working the weekend, but since moving here, she had a week's grace period before classes started to find another job. In the meantime, she'd enjoy sleeping in a few times.

She looked at her watch. Six am? Time to get back to sleep. It wasn't even light out yet, but then again, it was getting light later and later on these autumn days. Perhaps the sun would break through the windows in an hour or so. She snuggled closer under the duvet and closed her eyes, listening for birds and the sound of the wind. Those were the sounds she loved; out here, away from busy motorways, perhaps she would hear more of it again.

But there was another sound that dominated the soundscape. The sound of footsteps, soft but deliberate.
Perhaps one of the other girls wanted to go to the bathroom? She didn't move a muscle but looked toward the door she had left slightly ajar, eager to see if the cat would come to join her. To be honest, she was a big softie when it came to the animal. The thought of the cat calmed her a little right now.

The footsteps seemed to stop for a second before continuing, but now they moved up toward Ramona's room. She could feel her heart beating against her fingers as she pressed her hands to her chest. In theory, the other two did not need to come by her door to get to the bathroom. Maybe Valiant was looking for the cat, being quiet, in an effort to not wake the other girls. But something stopped her from calling out, eyes fixed on the little bit of hallway she could see in the semi-dark.

A shape moved past, definitely humanoid, and she had to stifle a gasp in her sheets. Luckily, it walked by so fast that it probably hadn't noticed her reaction, but Ramona could feel her stomach clench. Then there was... Nothing. Or was her heart pounding so hard in her ears that she just couldn't hear anything? Panic was spreading. The figure had been too tall and too dark to be one of the girls. There was something in this house—with them. But all the doors and windows had been locked. She had checked it herself.

At last, she kicked the sheets off and closed the distance to the door, throwing it open and looking around.

Nothing. The stairs were clear. Nothing seemed to have been moved. Had it been Ramona's imagination? A sighting of the ghost caused by her own telling of ghost stories? That'd be ironic. But wasn't that how ghost stories carried themselves on, anyway?

She could still feel her heart thudding in her chest as she circled the top floor before returning to her room.

Only under the safety of her blankets did she feel safe again. Her mind was still reeling, trying to form the image of what she had seen.

It seemed impossible. There wasn't anyone in the house that could have fit the description of what she had seen. Tall, dark, and somewhat... scary.

There was a soft meow beyond her headboard.
"Socks! It's not safe out there," she whispered and opened the blankets. The cat did not need any further coaxing. Socks jumped up and under the blankets with her, keeping his distance by staying near her feet. She sighed. What was that? Weren't cats supposed to be really good at keeping ghosts away? Okay, that was one of the reasons she had invited the cat into her bed. No harm, no foul, right? And warm feet to boost. She put her head down and closed her eyes, ready to drift back to sleep. She was trying to calm her heart and drift back to sleep when a draft of cold air told her the cat had vanished. Great, there went her hypothetical ghost shield.

Still, she kept her head down and soon dozed back off to sleep.

Chapter 7 – Ramona

Ramona's peaceful dreams were disturbed by the sound of a yell. For a groggy moment, she was blissfully forgetful of what she had seen earlier, but that didn't last long as the scream echoed through the house and brought back the memories of her early-morning ghost sighting.

She checked her phone. Ten am. Wince. She'd really slept in after that unfortunate moment. Footsteps thundered down the hall as someone else had clearly been awakened by the sounds. At last, she threw herself out of bed and rushed over.

George stood by Valiant's door, robe over her pajamas and hair wild around her face. Like a young Helena Bonham Carter, almost. *Strange to see her so awake*, Ramona thought. If left to her own devices, her friend could easily sleep until noon. Then again, Valiant was screaming her heart out.
"Val? Are you okay?" She finally pushed the ajar door open.
Valiant was standing on her bed, in the corner of the room, as far as she could get from Socks. Seeing the two girls, she pointed at the cat.
"Did he catch vermin? That's kind of his job, sweeth—" George paused as she saw what the cat was chewing on.

Ramona almost threw up. She turned away and swallowed hard.

"George. Tell me I'm not seeing things." She hid her face in her friend's shoulder. George remained remarkably calm.

"You are not delusional, dear." She patted her friend on the shoulder and slowly walked over to the cat. The little tuxedo cat was eagerly chewing on what looked to be a severed *human hand bone*.

Seeing her approach, Socks's ears flattened against his head, and he started growling lowly, backing away with his prize in his mouth.

"Valiant, I will need your assistance on this. We need to see what he's trying to eat."

Ramona blinked. "Well, as a biology student, I can tell you that most certainly looks like a bone, with mummified ski—"

Valiant shrieked at that.

"Yes, thank you, Ramona. Even as a humble liberal arts student, I could have told you that. But it looks…"

"Human," Ramona finished the sentence and rolled up her pajama sleeves. Valiant would not be much help. "What can I do? Wait! I need to get gloves!"

"Whatever for? He may be eating—well."

"Just in case. I don't know what that is!" She rushed to her room and grabbed her thick, marigold-yellow cleaning gloves. It took her a few tries to get them on properly as her hands were shaking, but she clapped her hands together once she had managed. "Alright!"

George sighed. "I'll grab the cat. You grab that chicken leg there."

"It's not a—"

"I know, but I also don't want to freak out Valiant even more. If you hadn't noticed, she is upset by all of this."

"Alright, alright. Let's do this."

George reached the cat with three confident strides and crouched over it, pushing down its butt and shoulders to keep it in place. Ramona grabbed the item and immediately stumbled back to ensure the cat couldn't get at her hands. The ordinarily docile Socks growled but settled down.

A deep sigh escaped Ramona's lips until she looked closer at the item in her hand.

"Call the police. This is from a human hand."

She wasn't sure what they'd thought it was, but she hoped against hope that maybe it was a chicken leg or a random kitchen leftover of some sort. But this was definitely a human hand. The bone song started playing in her head: ♫ *connected to the* ♫. **She turned it over**, recognizing it as a bone from the carpal bones in the base of the hand where it connected to the wrist. Some darkened, dried-up skin loosely hung off wasted flesh. She couldn't tell how old these remains were, but they were thin and dried out, at least ten years. There was no way this... Feeling a bit dizzy, she sat down on the floor.

She saw George pacing around the hallway with her phone in her hand. How was she so calm? Valiant had just completely curled up and was being comforted by Socks, who had already forgotten about the whole hand thing and licked her hand. He knew he would be fed soon anyway. *Perhaps that would get her out of her catatonia*, Ramona thought, not even aware she was herself experiencing a similar state of shock. Hah, *cat*-atonia.

49

"Come on. We need to find the body." George crouched down by her. "Come on."

"What?" Ramona looked down at her hand. "Oh. Oh god. I'm going to puke."

"Hang on." George rushed to her room to find a paper lunch bag and held it open.

"I think I can make it to the bathroom, George," Ramona protested.

"Not for that. Put the bone in here, so we don't have a repeat with Socks. Then we need to check the house. If this is here... who knows?"

She shivered, and Ramona realized she did not want any more of these kinds of surprises. She couldn't blame her. It seemed to have been just one thing after another as soon as they had moved into this house. Slowly, she dropped the bone into the bag, almost throwing up as she saw dried skin flakes drift to the floor. She quickly got all of it off her gloves and then stripped them off, throwing them into the trash. Sure, buying new ones was wasteful, but she did not want to see these gloves *ever* again.

She rushed to the bathroom. Heard George speaking softly to Valiant. She ran the water hot enough to turn her hands red and then washed them again. Three times before, they felt clean enough to dry off on her towel.

It was time to go... hunt for a corpse. *Fuck*. Laughing hoarsely to herself, seeing George enter the room. The young woman had changed out of her pajamas and into a pair of old-looking dungarees with a cutsew[3] underneath, probably the closest thing she had to work clothes.

"Good idea. Let me get some clothes on as well," she heard herself say softly.

Ramona had a pair of old jeans, a present from years ago she had kept, and a band shirt. She put them on and walked back over. Still no sign of Valiant.

"How's Valiant doing?"

"She's feeding Socks." George put on a hoodie over her top and shivered. "I think we should just check the attic quickly, just in case. Have you got any more torches?"

"Ah, yeah. I got a second one from camping." Sometimes, her biology course required her to go out into the wilderness in the dark. Torches, camping gear, and other unfashionable items of practicality had found their way into her stuff. She rushed back to her room, grabbed the crank torch, and hunted around the boxes, trying to remember where she had packed the damn battery torch.

At last, two torches in hand, she checked them for power, then walked back.

"You think she's okay?"

"Valiant? Yeah, she's focusing on Socks. Socks needs her right now, and she needs him, so that's a great interaction there." She

---

[3] Shirt made from stretch fabric with minor embellishments like buttons or lace. The term カットソー is a mixed word from the English terms "cut" and "sew". Outside the lolita fashion, it is a more typical simple shirt popular in Japan.

took one of the torches. "Wonderful. Thanks for your assistance on this."

Slowly, hearing that George was returning to her more relaxed, fancier speech, Ramona realized George probably had also been spooked by the whole thing but was just better at hiding it.

"Yeah…" Ramona grinned, looking around. "You know where the attic hatch is?"

"Yes. The small bedroom we've not used."

Ramona shivered. That tiny room had seemed foreboding and off-limits, but now they would have to go in.

She took the lead and pushed open the door to the place, sighing a little. "No skeletons in the closet," she quipped.

"But we haven't opened the—"

"It's a joke, George. Sorry," she muttered and walked into the room, turning on the ceiling light. There was still nothing here.

"Right, grab the reaching stick, please," George said while she looked up at the hatch toward the attic, absently pointing to a long wooden pole in the corner with a small brass hook on its end. The oversized pool cue was typically in older houses to open high windows and creepy entrances to old attics.

Being a bit taller than George, Ramona hooked the stick into the ring at the end of the hatch and pulled it down. A smell of dust came down, and the ladder was folded up neatly. George unclasped it and let the bottom part of the ladder slide to the ground, making sure it was stable before climbing up.

Reluctantly, Ramona followed after her. There was very little room on the thin ladder, and it didn't seem the strongest, so she let George go first before following her.

"If anything is out here, please shut up forever," Ramona muttered as she climbed the last bit.

"Shut up, please," George sighed, a little bit grumpy. Then again, Ramona could understand. This morning, they'd dealt with a lot between Valiant's screaming and finding human remains in their brand new residence.

Residence. Now Ramona definitely knew she was spending too much time with George. Talking all uppity and fancy-like, very middle class. If they weren't up here to find a dead body, that kind of thing would crack her up immensely.

"Let's have a gander," said George, turning 360 degrees with the torch on.

Ramona did the same, looking around as the beam of light hit the rafters and the various boxes and things around them.

It all looked pretty undisturbed, but Ramona had only inspected it briefly when they were shown the house. The attic lacked the usual left-behind boxes and disused furniture that was usual for lofts and tucked-away corners. It was empty, with the dust piling up around the rafters.

Pretty normal. If this house had been built for someone who had never lived in it, they wouldn't have had the chance to fill it. And it seemed any resident since had not bothered to put things up here. Perhaps none of them had stayed long enough.

"Ramona," George's voice got her out of her reverie. "I don't like it up here."

Ramona nodded. She got the same vibe.

"Hang on, what's that?" She looked over to the far end, deep in the dark, near where the rafters met the window. It looked like... you couldn't call it a coffin. It was too roughly made, a casket crafted from rough, untreated wooden planks nailed together.

"No way."

George sounded, well, less than surprised. "Was this here when you inspected the house?"

Ramona blinked. "I honestly can't say. I just had a look around real quick, that's all."

"So... Should we..." Ramona closed her eyes briefly. "Alright. Let's open it."

To her surprise, George beat her to the casket. She moved fast and quietly, even though it felt like Ramona couldn't move an inch without making the wood creak.

"Help me lift this, and be careful of splinters," said George.

It made her dizzy to realize that they might find a dead body in there, but she had to push on. She carefully grabbed the lid and nodded to George, who started to shove the lid off the casket with a single push.

More dust as the lid dropped to the ground with a thud. It almost cracked, but George caught it on the second bounce. It was definitely old and stained but in good condition.

"Alright. You can look away." George looked over to Ramona, and there was no judgment in her eyes. No fear or trepidation either, which confused Ramona. *How could she be so calm about all of this?*

"No. I'm the biologist." She cleared her throat. "Just. Give me a moment." She nodded, then carefully looked into the box. "Oh god."

The remains were old and dried out but definitely human. The form stretched out the length of the rough casket wasn't very tall, with the pelvis hinting at a male. It was mostly bones, with blackened-looking skin tensed over it. Dark-brown hair curled gingerly over the forehead mixed in with spiderwebs, making the whole thing somehow look even worse. The clothes were rotted away for the most part and seemed to have consisted of a straightforward attire with little structure. Almost like a shroud, but not quite.

"Do you think we found Adam Lockhart?" George blinked.

Ramona shook her head.

"Didn't he die in battle? Why would they ship him back here and then put him in his own attic?" She shook her head.

"We need to call the police." George shook her head. "Fuck. We found a body." She almost laughed nervously.

"Right." Ramona looked at the ladder. "I'll go... call... you..."

"You go," George encouraged her. "I'll come in a second. I'll just put the lid back, so the cat doesn't jump in or something. It looks like it could be very fragile, and if Socks already got in..." She took a deep breath.

Ramona peeked back. The body was indeed missing a hand, which made her shiver. "Yeah... Imagine." The tiny predator could do a lot of damage. "He looks burned. What happened here?"

He definitely couldn't have burned in the casket—the casket was flammable. But to put a burned body into the coffin would have been quite a task and practically impossible without breaking it. This was just such a weird thing to have happened. Why? Who found bodies in their new rentals? This was so out of this world.

She rushed toward the ladder and slung herself down to go locate her phone. With shaky fingers, she dialed the emergency line and explained what had been going on. Well, she told them about the body. All the other stuff about seeing things wasn't too useful right now. Right now, she focused on the most pressing matter: There was a dead body in her attic, and she had no idea how it got there. The owner would probably have to be told, but that was a worry for another time.

The person on the other end of the line remained calm, letting her know what to do. At long last, George came down the ladder, went into her room briefly to check her phone, and then went back up before coming down again. She seemed as restless as Ramona was feeling, constantly biting her fingernails and unable to sit down for very long. Her stoic friend was feeling rattled, she could tell.

The operator remained on the line until she could see the police car approaching from the front porch. She needed fresh air. Valiant had gotten dressed in some jean shorts and an old heavy-metal band shirt and was carrying Socks around, busying herself with the cat.

"You guys found the rest of the body?" she asked softly, and George nodded before Ramona could reply.

"Yeah, let's just say... It's best you didn't see," Ramona followed up and stood up as the police van arrived as well as an ambulance, likely to take the body with them. She glanced up as George joined them outside, a parasol overhead as the sun was starting to rise. She really was committed to the whole aesthetic.

"Hi. I'm Ramona. I called," she greeted the officers who came up to the house. "It... He's in the attic." She cleared her throat and led them inside after George, who closed the parasol and put it away. It was such a strange thing to see her with a parasol for such a brief moment. The officer was talking to her softly and then followed her up the ladder to the casket.

Their torches were a lot brighter than her own, and she had to blink to get used to the light.

"No power up here?" one of them asked, a tall man who had to stoop in the small attic.

"Not really, no," Ramona said. "I mean, I haven't found the plugs, and no light sockets were set up."

Perhaps a good thing—this thing would probably be billed as an extra bedroom had it had a window.

"Right." The officer looked around. "In there?" he said as the beam of light hit the casket.

"Yes," Ramona said softly and heard them put on gloves before they walked over. Had these people seen many dead bodies before? If they had, had they been in this horrid kind of state?

"Miss. Can you come over, please?" The tall one looked over to her after taking the lid off.

What a strange request, she thought, but she walked over anyway.

"Mmm?"

"Come have a look," the officer invited.

"Do I have to?" She made a face, but when she looked down, she blinked. "Oh."

57

The bones were gone. Some rags lay in its place, similar to the clothes the body had worn—the same roughly hewn cotton.

"Are you sure you saw a body?"

"Yes, there was a skull, a pelvis, and all the bits in between and below." She resisted the temptation to lift up the fabric, and the policeman picked up the material.

"Right. Seems like you let shadows trick you, miss." The officer put the lid back on. "This thing is quite old but probably best made into some firewood. Can't have this kind of thing scaring the next person. Or as one of those vintage Halloween decorations."

"Hallow—" She shook her head. "Sir, I know what I saw. It was a body!"

"But there's no body here right now. So, we'll be going, and if you do find anything, please let us know."

There was little left of the earlier warmth she'd heard in the voice, and she followed them toward the ladder again.

Where had it gone? Had it been a trick of the light? She absently mopped up something wet near the ladder, blinking at the strange smell. Blood?

She turned her touch to her hand and blinked. "That's…"

The officer turned to her. "Strange. Are you hurt?" he asked, and she shook her head.

"Perhaps someone got a splinter coming up here. Go on down first," he said, letting her go down. "You girls should be careful in a big house like this."

George looked up as they came down. "What— where's the body?"

"There is no body, miss. I'm thinking it was a trick of the light. First day in the new house?"

58

Valiant nodded. "Yeah... but..." She put down Socks and rushed into her room to grab the bag with the bone in it.

Yes! At least they had that for evidence. The officer looked into the bag and frowned. "That's... Definitely something. Where was this found?"

"Well." Valiant looked away. "I woke up to my cat trying to eat it," she simply said. "But... I don't know how he got it."

"Could he get up to the attic?" The other officer put on gloves and transferred the contents carefully into an evidence bag.

"I don't think so. But... he's a cat. They get anywhere you don't want them to go."

"That's pretty much true." The officer smiled politely. "Thank you. We will have this analyzed, and if it does turn out to be human, we may need to search the premises for the... rest of the remains." Ramona laughed nervously. "Yeah," she said and looked over. "Thank you for coming out. I know it's quite a way..."

"Not a problem, miss. Not like we need to walk." Still, the officer didn't seem quite as happy as he was trying to sound. Perhaps he was frustrated that this was all that they had come out for—a single hand bone.

Still, she was glad that it hadn't vanished because it would have been even harder to explain all of this. Where had the body gone? Without the hand bone, she could have imagined they had just hallucinated it, maybe seen sticks looking like a skeleton.

This fucking house. Was it another apparition?

She shook her head and walked over to Valiant, who was walking the officer out to the front door.

"This is a very big house. You lock it up right at night?" the one officer asked.

"Yeah. We're getting an alarm as well," Ramona said, though she wasn't sure why. Though she had to admit she was considering it at this point. So much strange stuff had happened.

"An alarm might be a good idea. Just in case. Someone might have been using the house while it was empty, and they might not have figured out this place is being lived in again."

She nodded, looking around for the other two.

George stood by the stairs, arms crossed. She seemed a bit freaked out by all of this; she hadn't spoken in a while. Valiant was slowly regaining some color, at least, now that the bone was out of her life and no body had been found.

Maybe it had just been some weird coincidence. People held onto the most bizarre things. But how did it get here? She saw the police and the ambulance off before walking back inside.

Valiant was still a bit pale. George rubbed her hands.

"I'm making tea. Anyone want any?" George asked.

Valiant nodded, and despite her usual dislike of tea, Ramona nodded too. She knew there was so much more to tea than just the tea itself; it was a thing for her English friends to congregate around.

George poured some of her lovely loose-leaf into a pot and sighed, looking at the both of them as the electric kettle worked its magic. It must have been the first thing she unpacked.

Valiant bit her lip. "I'm going to spend today unpacking, I think. I keep thinking about…" Her look toward Socks told Ramona all she needed to know.

"Agreed," said George. "I want to have the kitchen sorted out, at least, so if you have any bits for here, just bring them over here."

"Were you serious about the alarm?" asked Valiant.

"Not really. I don't know. What do you guys think?"

"It's a lot of money, and I don't think it's necessary out here," George said. "If the landlord wants it, okay, but I definitely don't want it installed on my dime."

"I agree," said Ramona. "I just… Don't feel all that safe out here with just the locks."

"Honestly, it's fine. I'm sure that…"

"I saw something this morning," Ramona piped up. "Six am or so. Something passed by my door. Something way taller than you guys."

Something… about as tall as the body in the attic had been. She wasn't sure why that suddenly came up in her brain, but it was true.

Valiant blinked. "What? How— What happened?"

"It just… walked by the door. That's all. I went out to see where it went off to, but it looked to have vanished. Then Socks came out of nowhere. I let him into my room, but he soon ran off again."

"Sounds like Socks," Valiant admitted. "And you're sure it wasn't just a shadow or something?"

"No! It was tall and dark!" Only then did she realize how much that sounded like a shadow. "I… It looked tangible. The light didn't pass through it." She licked her lips. "I know it's weird. But

61

after the noises yesterday, I don't know." She rubbed her forehead.

George grabbed the boiling kettle and poured the water over the leaves in the pot.

"I believe you," she said simply. And Ramona realized that that was just what she wanted to hear.

"Thank you." Ramona closed her eyes briefly. Weird ritual or not, the tea smelled terrific.

"I haven't got any milk, but this oolong should be fine without it," she said simply.

"Oolong? Nice." Valiant smiled a little. "I love Oolong."

"I know." George smiled. "You got me this one for my birthday."

Ramona smiled a little. It really helped to have her friends here, even if this situation was bizarre. She held her hands up. "Right. Unpacking sounds good today. After tea. And if any skeletons pop up, don't let me know." She winked.

"Will do." George grinned, pouring three cups of tea. "But first. Tea." She carried the two mugs over to the dining table and then walked back to get her own.

"I'm still not sold on this big kitchen..." She shook her head. "I like having the door closed when I cook."

"You can still do that. It's just that the dining room is also included in the space," said Valiant. A quarter of the floorplan of the ground floor was basically a pantry, kitchen and dining room, with only two doors to separate it from the study, which formed another quarter. Then the eastern half of the ground floor created the expansive lounge. The large common areas had attracted them because it meant the first floor was basically just bedrooms, which really made sure they all had their own space, but also room to host meets[4].

"Alright. So, we've got a possibly haunted house, with a strange ghost, a disappearing corpse, a bonkers cat…. Am I missing anything?" Valiant laughed and looked around, curling her fingers around the cup of tea.

"Sounds about right," Ramona agreed. "At least we can take your car to speed out of here. Unless the gas—petrol, I mean—gets drained."

"Hah, good joke. It's a hybrid." She laughed and looked over. "Like I'd drive a petrol car."

"What was I thinking?" Ramona grinned. "Still, it means we have options, even if it's living in a hybrid for a term while we find another house."

"Oh, gods, no." George laughed. "I like living big. I'd rather move back in with my mother." She rolled her eyes and sipped the tea.

"Oh, heck no. I'd take the car over moving back home." Ramona laughed, sipping her cup as well and feeling soothed by the warm tea.

Valiant shook her head. "At least my family isn't that terrible."

"It's not about horrible families, sweetie. I like… being independent of them." Ramona shrugged. "I'm an adult, you know. I don't want to rely on them forever."

---

[4] Meets or meet-ups are gatherings of people into lolita fashion as a hobby. To show off dresses, celebrate the hobby, see friends, and enjoy side activities such as high tea or swap meets to buy and sell dresses.

Valiant nodded. "I guess. I mean, I know my family will be there for me forever." She smiled.

"Though, oh my gosh, my mum still thinks she can cook, and it's simply not true. I told her I had turned vegetarian so I could avoid her overcooked steak."

George laughed behind a daintily held-up hand. "I'm glad we have a cook, honestly."

"Where did you learn to cook then?" Valiant blinked. Her friend spent most nights in the kitchen.

"Oh, you know, I look things up. I use those meal delivery boxes. I just get them delivered once a week and then use those. They're good and healthy and all that. It's kind of like... crafting with tiny food boxes."

"Wow, that's so middle class. I mean..." Ramona sighed. *Thinking before speaking, damn it.*

Luckily, George just laughed. "I guess so. But it's easy!"

"I bet, but even so..." Ramona shook her head. "It feels like Kraft Mac & Cheese boxes, but way more expensive."

"Yeah, I guess so. But not that much more expensive than groceries, to be honest." George sipped her tea. "Either way, it is just a preference."

Ramona nodded. "So, I think we should get unpacking." She curled her fingers around the mug. This was nice, though. Better than running around. After all that had happened today... She shook her head. And it wasn't even noon.

Valiant nodded. "Agreed. I want to do groceries at some point today."

"I'll be in. My prep boxes should be delivered today," said George.

"I'll join you for groceries, and then we can take the car. I mean, if that's okay with you." Ramona looked over to Valiant.

"Yeah, duh." Valiant laughed. "That's what it's there for. The buses here are kind of crap, unfortunately… part of why my parents gave me the car."

"And it's quite a way into town. Maybe doable on a bike, though."

"Ew, bikes." George made a face. "I'll just Uber there if I need to." She shook her head.

"Anyway. Let's get on with it," said Ramona. "Thanks so much for the tea, George. This really helped."

They'd needed something to pull themselves together.

"Okay." Valiant nodded and finished her cup. "I'll head into town at two pm. If anyone wants to come for groceries, head down to the hall. Send me a text if you want anything specific but don't wanna come."

She shrugged. "As long as you don't need me to buy you furniture."

Chapter 8 – Ramona

Time seemed to have flown by while they were unpacking. Ramona had just gotten her desk and books sorted when she heard Valiant call up.

"Food run! All who want to join, get your butts down," she said, this time dressed for the occasion in a simple JSK[5] with cutsew and patterned tights to match. "Someone please come with me because, damn, small town."

Ramona walked down. She'd kept her outfit from this morning on to be comfy. "Small town?"

"Everyone will want to know why the police were here. You know. Why did the new people in the supposedly haunted house need the cops?"

Ramona swallowed. "Oh."

"Yeah," said Valiant, grabbing her totes.

Ramona sighed and grabbed her backpack. The atmosphere in the house had brightened, but it would still be hard to explain the morning's events to others.

"What do we tell people?" George stood in the doorway to the kitchen.

"Well, that we found some remains and called the police. The vanishing skeleton does not need to be part of the narrative,"

---

[5] Style of dress without sleeves. The term comes from an abbreviation of jumper skirt.

Valiant said. "I mean. It's… Just not relevant, and we probably shouldn't comment too much on an ongoing investigation."

"That's a good line," said Ramona. "George, do you want anything?"

"Nah. Just text me if there's a good tea shop anywhere," George replied before retreating into the kitchen.

Ramona nodded. "Alright! Don't do anything we wouldn't. We'll be back soon!"

Valiant grinned. "She should probably be more worried about us than we are about her," she said. "I mean, we're the ones seeing things."

"Yeah, but they're real!" Ramona closed the door behind them. "I mean. We aren't seeing things. I mean, we are, but…" She sighed. "I think there's something in that house. Maybe a ghost that wants us to find its remains. Maybe something else."

Valiant shook her head. "I'm not so sure about any of this, to be honest. Maybe it wasn't even a human bone, and we got all flustered about a burned chicken leg."

"Chicken leg?" Ramona paused her walk to the car. "What— you know the Halloween kids? What if the chicken leg was just some burned chicken leg the pranksters that day left behind?"

Valiant looked over. "You think that bone could have been…"

"Maybe. A human hand bone can be similar in size to a big chicken bone. What if… it was just that?"

This time, Valiant laughed out loud. "You mean we called the police on some kind of chicken bone?" She grinned and unlocked the car with her key. "That would be hilarious. I can't wait to hear back from the police. Excuse me, you've got a deceased chicken on your property. We have a warrant."

"That's a terrible impersonation of a cop. And sounded more like an American one!"

"Well, I'm sorry, does it look like I have a lot of experience with the police? I've never gotten into much trouble." She grinned.

"Speaking of trouble, we've got a meet tomorrow." Ramona looked up from her phone.

"Ah yeah. I hope I'm finished unpacking by then because I had a whole outfit planned," Valiant said. "I'm so behind with YouTube videos as well."

"I wouldn't worry too much about that. We can make a video with the three of us once we're up and running and do one of those cute 'what we've been up to' videos." Ramona smiled. She wasn't as big into the YouTube thing as her friends, but she wasn't exactly the most prolific on social media either. Valiant had a large following on Instagram and YouTube, George had some very successful unboxing videos and shop reviews, but Ramona had never found her niche. Usually, she made videos about meets and some releases, but they were never really successful. To be honest, she preferred spending time on her other hobbies, like reading.

None of the girls had ever looked at her strangely for that, which was why she loved them so much.

"Wow, this car really is nice." Ramona slipped into the seat, not believing the new car smell. Even that seemed more expensive and refined in this one.

"Yeah, I love it!" Valiant grinned. "I wanted the pink one, but dad said that that was a bit over the top for a car you're meant to have a few years at least, so I went with something more neutral."

She started up the car and backed up slowly out of the driveway.

"That's a pretty good shout, to be honest." She looked around as they got away from the house.

"Yeah, I guess, but I want to be Kawaii till I die," she sighed and carefully took to the road. "At least it's good to have a car, you know? I could not imagine living out here and having to rely on buses."

"That's the thing. I really need to buy myself an old clunker or something."

Ramona sat back. "If you'd told me years ago I'd be over eighteen and not have a car, I wouldn't have believed you. It's just so un-American!" She shook her head as they left the driveway.

Finally, the fields and forests made way for stores and the townscape. After fifteen more minutes, they pulled up at the local Tesco and parked in the parking lot. Ramona stretched as she got out and checked she had her bags and purse on her.

"Alright. Let's get some grub!" She grinned, quite excited to do the shopping for the first week in the new house. The essentials like spices and pasta had been packed, but she couldn't wait to do some simple cooking. An omelet sounded perfect for tonight.

Valiant nodded. "And our new fridge is sooo big!" She groaned and grabbed a shopping cart. "We'll finally all have room for our stuff!"

Ramona already noticed some looks about their outfits, but that was pretty on par for the course.

"That's such a nice thing," Ramona sighed. "I can't wait to fill it. It'll really make the house feel like a home to cook."

Though the thought of some random weirdo making fried chicken in their kitchen still confused her. Why chicken? It seemed like a complicated and unexpected dish to make just to scare some kids.

"You're thinking of the fried chicken again, aren't you?" Valiant guessed, and she nodded.

"Yeah. It just doesn't make sense, you know? And how's it linked to what I saw? Or is it just... coincidence, all three times something happened?"

"Well, I guess we'll just have to wait and see, to be honest," Valiant said. "Maybe there won't be anything else happening, and in a month, we'll realize that it was just all ridiculous nonsense."

Ramona laughed and grabbed a loaf of bread. "I really hope so. I'll take the front of the cart for my stuff?"

"Yeah, sounds good."

Valiant looked over the cookies and decided on some shortbread biscuits to treat herself.

"Let's go." She made her way past the meal-deal stuff and toward the fresh fruit and veg as Ramona tried to let go of the confusion in her brain.

Chapter 9 - Ramona

"Ramonaaa! Have you seen my hoop skirt? Did you give it back after you borrowed it?" came Valiant's voice.

"Yeah! Remember? I brought it along in the move and put it in your room."

"Right... Oh! You folded it up all small, wow!" Valiant called from her room. "Sorry!"

"All good. Just be careful when you unpa—" There was a thump as the hoop skirt exploded from the cramped packaging.

"Valiant, you okay?" Ramona shouted out.

Valiant groaned. "All good! Not the first time I got hit in the face with a hoop skirt."

Ramona finished her smoky-eye makeup and got up from her newly set up beauty desk. Did she want to wear a wig today? She pulled at a curl and sighed, then gave it a careful combing, put it in a top knot and wrapped a braided section around the base. That should keep it looking okay for the day, at least.

She picked out her dress for the day—a Moitie OP she had been saving just for a meet like this. With her Roland jacket over it and the right accessories, it formed the perfect outfit for this meet. Classy and gothic to meet her mood.

She checked her overall coord[6], walking out into the hallway, her skirt bouncing energetically as she called out.

"Guys, we need to be gone in five!"

A slightly panicked shriek answered from Valiant's room. "I almost got my lashes on!"

George strode out, eyes rolling back with her head as she heard Valiant's comment. George was wearing a black Metamorphose OP with the matching brand stockings and bonnet originally sold with the dress. Fancy.

"At least you're ready," said Ramona as she admired George's coord.

"Yes, but I'm not driving us there," George quipped as she picked her parasol up and finished the outfit with some sunglasses. "I won't miss summer, jeeze." Her skin glistened thick with sunscreen.

"Well, you know how English summers are. It'll last all of three weeks, and then we'll be back to freezing our butts off in the rain."

"This is true."

At long last, Valiant casually walked out in her sax-colored Fancy Paper Dolls JSK with a pink blouse and pink shoes. Valiant had accessorized her outfit with light-blue ankle socks, a pink head bow, diamante lashes and impressively teased high pigtails in her hair. Her pigtails also had little sparkly accessories as a finishing detail. At least she looked good for the time she took.

"Right! Let's go." Valiant smiled and walked down the stairs as if she had been waiting for them.

---

[6] In lolita fashion, a coord, short for coordinate, is a coordinated outfit including shoes.

Ramona grinned and walked down the stairs to follow her friend, with George following last in the vanguard, the one to close the ranks.

After an uneventful drive to the meet, they got out of the car. The Greenwich Maritime museum and the surrounding park were popular spots for lolita meet-ups—the park itself was vast and beautiful, and it was usually pretty easy to get to, being located by the river with connections by road, tube, and train.

It felt to Ramona as if they were this badass squad. The goths protecting their cute sweet lolita. The reality was, of course, much less impressive as they scrambled to grab headpieces, parasols, and picnic baskets out of the car.

Valiant locked up the car and walked to the picnic site. Everyone was gathered in a ring of blankets. It was a warm fall day, and it was best to enjoy the last echoes of summer while they lasted.

Ramona found a spot in the shade and put down her blanket as people came over to say hi and offer customary hugs and greetings. George especially was well known in this part of the comm and got a lot of hugs, excited greetings, and utterances about how they hadn't seen her in forever.

Ramona took the last bits out of her bag, placed them on her blanket, and looked up as her friend Brendon sat by her.

"Hey, handsome." She grinned. "How have you been?"

Brendon nodded. "Pretty good. Roland, huh? Aren't you too warm?"

Ramona fingered her body-length winter coat from Atelier Boz, its sharp edges and rounded brass buttons forming a lovely contrast.

"Not too hot for the aesthetic." She grinned. "You should see our new house! It's brilliant!" She finished unpacking her finger foods. "I intend to come over! We need to have a proper housewarming party!" Brendon was always the outgoing type, and she loved that about him.

But the idea of a housewarming party kind of scared the shit out of her right now. Her mind started racing with the implications of having her friends group over at the house... What if the shadowy figure showed up again?

"Ramona? Are you okay?"

She blinked, realizing she had zoned out, lost in her terror.

"Yeah! Yeah. Housewarming, yeah. Oh no, is—" She groaned, seeing a new figure walking proudly across a new dress. "Kayla got Khronos Utopia."

"Yeah, she was talking about—"

"She's wearing it right now," Ramona hissed through her teeth, looking over Brendon's shoulder.

Brendon tried to peek behind himself without showing.

"Oh shit. George has been wanting that one for ages, hasn't she?"

"Yup." Ramona cleared her throat. "This is going to be interesting... George said the listing she had an eye on got sniped..."

Brendon grinned in mischievous enjoyment.

"Oh, no way. She's going to get murdered." He laughed and shook his head a little. "She wouldn't have sniped someone's listing for a dress... Hi, George."

George sat down by them. "I can't believe her. She sniped me!" she huffed, tearing open a pack of crisps. "I complimented her, and she said she got it from the Italian reseller. I was following the listing!"

"There, there." Brendon padded her on the back. "There'll be other opportunities. And you know the Italian seller is super overpriced."

"Thanks. I so wish I hadn't slept on this dress."

Ramona sighed. "Yeah... don't we all?" She shook her head. "Man. I'm sorry, babe."

"Thanks." George rolled into the shade and sighed. "I can't wait for her to sell it on. Gonna bookmark her sales profile." George closed her parasol and briefly aimed it at Kayla as if she was aiming a rifle.

Ramona put her hand on the umbrella rifle, lowering it.

"It'll come up for sale again, and you know Angelic Pretty, they'll probably re-release it," said Ramona with a chuckle before diving her hand into the bag of crisps and taking out a handful of crisps for herself.

"At least she looks good in it," George admitted, lying down on her front. "Can we go to the pub yet?"

Ramona looked at her watch. They'd shown up about half an hour after the meet started, which was pretty standard. It was now four pm, and she knew the meet would begin to wind down around five.

"If you can last another half hour, we can invite the host along to the pub and make a dignified exit," Ramona guesstimated.

George nodded.

"Fine. Just wake me up when this spot is in danger of no longer being shady."

"I'm here, and it's always going to be shady." Brendon winked. "By the way, I need to send you that headdress."

"You finished it?" George's head shot up.

"Yes, at long last."

"Then what are we waiting for? Let's go to the pub so I can buy you a drink!" She sat up and grinned.

"Fine! Let me go say bye to people and invite them along." Ramona threw her hands up with a dramatic sigh.

"What if we go to a pub close to your house?" asked Brendon. "Then I can see your house?"

Ramona thought about it for a second. It would be a lot cheaper than a London pub, that was for sure. "Yeah, sure! We've got a space in the car, but you'll have to get home from there."

"Or crash at your place like the hot hobo I am." Brendon winked and sat back.

George rolled onto her back. "We have a guest room and a ghost. You'll fit right in."

"Don't tell people about that shit. We don't know what it is," Ramona said with a frown.

"We're pretty sure the house is haunted," George clarified, shrugging. "Not sure by what."

Brendon seemed taken aback.

"No kidding. Alright. Still good with this." He shrugged.

George frowned briefly at that but soon lit up again. "Alright then. Let's extract Valiant from the sweet territory and go." She made a few half-hearted attempts at getting up.

"Fine, I shall vacate the shade and go." Ramona grinned and got up. At least the sun was starting to wane, and the Indian summer heat was letting up. It had been a beautiful September day. She waded over to Valiant and sat down. She still managed to stand out in the group of pastel-clad lolitas.

One of the standouts in the group was Lara. She was wearing a beautiful Baby The Stars Shine Bright[7] JSK and matching socks with an embroidered blouse. Headwear-wise, she had gone with a beautiful flower crown. At the end of her waist-length brown braids, she had small flower ribbon combs that matched the entire outfit.

Ramona caught herself staring. "Daaamn. Is that Polonaise Brillante?"

Lara smiled. "Hey. Yes! I just got it. I love it."

"It looks amazing on you. That apron is… chef's kiss, honestly," Ramona groaned. "You're gonna make me want to go down the road of an entirely new sub-style[8]."

"I'm sure you could pull off country." She smiled.

"Aw, you're too kind… Hi, Kayla. Looking great." Ramona turned to the other lolita next to her.

"Thanks. Though if George kills me, please tell the police."

---

[7] One of the most popular lolita brands, specialising in sweet and classic designs. Also the cause of Usakumya addiction, where sufferers hoard dysphoric teddy bears that pretend to be rabbits. I promise it makes sense.

[8] Lolita has several sub-styles. The main ones are sweet, gothic, and classic. Others include pirate, country, hime, punk…

"It's not that bad." Ramona grinned. "She'll get over it. Listen, we were thinking of heading to the pub. It's that kinda time."

"Yeah!" Valiant unplugged her phone from her Hello Kitty charger and started hugging the girls around her. The queen of the cute little clique.

"You're invited, by the way. We're going to the pub in the town near our new house. Brendon might stay the night."

She directed the last part at Valiant, who nodded.

"Sounds great. You know he's just gonna turn it into a party, right?"

"That's what he always does." She shrugged. Some of the others were starting to pack up and go, winding the energy of the meet down. Picnic blankets were being picked up and shaken out, treats divided, and baskets packed.

It had been a lot of fun.

"Alright." Valiant shooed her clique off her picnic blanket and gave it a brush and shake before folding it up.

"Had fun?" asked Ramona, and Valiant nodded.

"Yeah. You goths had fun as well in the shade?" She stuck her tongue out.

"Sure did." Ramona winked and helped fold Valiant's blanket before packing it into the basket. George strode over from the shade; her large parasol and shades were covering most of her. Waving, George called out as she walked.

"Kayla! You should join us!"

Kayla chuckled nervously. "Sure thing. How's it going?"

"Pretty good. That's such a cute dress." George looked over it from top to bottom.

"I had no idea that was your username bidding on it, promise," Kayla blurted out.

"Sweetie. Stop stressing. It's fine," George said in sweet tones, shaking her head. "Should I worry I have this effect on people? I won't... Whatever, it's all good."

Ramona relaxed a little as the tension drained. For a moment there, she thought there would be a fight.

"I'll join for the pub." It seemed more like Kayla wanted to show George she wasn't afraid more than anything else.

"Alright, let's go say bye to Estelle," Ramona said, sighing and looking around for the young woman who had organized the meet. Estelle was very good at managing these meets, so it was always a pleasure to be invited to one of her gatherings.

Estelle was picking up her trash and looked over as Ramona and Valiant approached.

"Hi, you both! Had fun?"

"Yeah." Valiant smiled. "Thank you so much for organizing, I had a great time. And, you know, next time, I'm bringing cake!" she said. There had been no time to bake yet, but even Ramona was looking forward to some lovely cake. Valiant was so good at making them, and it would make the house smell and feel even more like home.

Estelle hugged them both. "Well, thanks for coming. I can't wait for the big tea party later this month."

"Oh, my gosh, same. I need to find an outfit," Valiant squeed. "Maybe go very OTT sweet, 2010s style. Aaah!" She grinned a little, and Ramona chuckled.

"Yes, we will see you there. We're going to the pub closer to our place if you want to join, but we've run out of room in the car," said Valiant.

"That's alright. I'm going to collapse a bit and sleep through tomorrow." Estelle grinned. "Have fun, though." She waved and saw them both off.

Packing the blankets into the car, Valiant smiled. "Also, have I mentioned how handy the car is?"

The five of them squeezed into the car before heading off. It was a bit tight, but it was quite a fun ride. Valiant was as outgoing as always, having a lot of fun talking to her friends and filling the silence for the more exhausted introverts in the front. Ramona peeked into the back from time to time, but Kayla and Brendon were still happy with George squeezed in the middle.

George just leaned her head back, joining the conversation from time to time.

"Finally, we're here!" The sun was just starting to set as they drove onto the pub's parking lot, and all got out.

"We've not gone to this pub yet, but we hear it's the best..."

"The only one," George interrupted.

"The best one in town," Valiant continued. "And we can get dinner here because there's no way I'm cooking for all of you."

"That's fair enough." Kayla grinned and straightened out her skirt. "I am so craving a greasy burger and fries after all the sweet food at the picnic."

"Agreed," said Brendon. "My devilled eggs always go so fast. I think I only had half of one myself." He chuckled and opened the door. "Ladies first."

The pub had the usual smell of wood and stale beer, but it was clean and cooling after the warmth of the park. The lights were low, thanks to the small windows and the mood lighting. It was every pub Ramona had ever visited in this country. They were such lovely places, especially the older ones in central London. The town and country ones tended to be bigger and well-tended, but... sometimes just more modern. It had a whole different feel to the ones she had discovered the first few nights sneaking out of her parents' house.

"Let's find a table." George walked toward the quieter corner, where there were fewer people.
Ramona grabbed a few menus from the adjacent tables and handed them to the others on the table.
Ramona looked at the menu, but she knew what she was getting: the burger with a coke. Every pub did their own versions, so she was spoiled for choice, but today really just was a bacon cheeseburger kind of day. Valiant went with a vegetarian cheese and bean wrap, and George just wanted a rum and coke. Probably had snacked too much at the meet. Brendon picked a pizza, while Kayla went with a burger as well.

"This seems like a great town," said Brendon, looking around. A few families had joined for a Saturday night dinner, and a pair of girlfriends were sharing a bottle of wine and catching up. Random bits of boyfriend-related conversation could be heard whenever the table fell silent.

"So, what's the deal with the house?" Brendon asked, and George groaned.

"It's haunted. We told you, didn't we?" She shrugged and looked over to Valiant and Ramona.

Valiant grinned sheepishly. "It's not that bad, promise. It's... We've had some... occurrences... but... Ah."

"We don't know what it is," Ramona said after deciding to go with soda rather than any alcoholic. The one thing this country did right—pint-sized cokes.

"There's definitely something in the house. Possibly a ghost." She shivered at the memory of the ghost walking by her door. Was it a ghost? It had seemed so much more tangible than a specter. A walking corpse? She blinked at the thought, immediately dismissing it as ridiculous.

"Now I definitely need to stay over." Brendon grinned, looking around at the others.

Kayla rolled her eyes. "You do that. I want to get home before midnight, so I'll get going once we've finished dinner. Thanks for the invite, though, but even if there's such a thing as ghosts, I don't want to see them."

"There's definitely such a thing." George looked over. "Simply ignoring their existence will not stop them from existing."

The table quietened down a moment before Brendon piped up.

"Buuuullshit," he simply said. "There's science behind why people think they see or hear ghosts. And a lot of those conditions are compounded when you're in an older house."

"I saw things, okay?" Ramona frowned. "You come spend the night and tell me I'm fucking around." She crossed her arms, and the discussion fell silent again.

"George. Let's go order," she finally said, still a bit upset with George. It seemed like the other girl was trying to wind everyone up about the ghost. She had to know everyone would want to challenge it, especially Brendon, who was a scientist.

"What's your problem?" she asked at the bar.

The bargirl raised an eyebrow, and Ramona groaned. "Sorry. Not you, my friend over here."

"Right. Do you want a moment, or are you ready to order?"

"Double rum and coke for me," said George, not giving Ramona the time to get back to the topic at hand.

Now a little destabilized, she sighed and shook her head.

"Cheeseburger with bacon. Fries and a large coke, please," she said, and the bar girl noted down their order and table number.

"Why are you almost daring these two to come to our house?" she asked, gentler this time.

"I'm just stating my opinion. There is something in this house." George looked over. "That is an undeniable fact."

"Perhaps, but... it makes us sound like we're insane." And that was really it. Nobody really believed in ghosts, so to say that stuff outright... She shook her head.

George did something Ramona had rarely seen her do. She shrugged and paid for her drink when it came.

"I'll let the others know to come and order," she simply said and walked back to the table, apparently not bothered by the fact she had just been rudely called on her bullshit.

Ramona let out a low growl and threw her head back.

"You need a drink as well?" asked the bar lady, looking over.

"No, just the coke, please. But thanks."

"You guys are up in the Lockhart house?" the girl asked, filling a large glass with coke. The spout fizzed loudly, and it always fascinated Ramona.

"Yeah. Just moved in. I didn't realize it had a name?" She blinked, realizing what the girl had called it.

"Oh yeah, we call it the Lockhart house, after the guy who commissioned it. The tragic soldier story and all that. That sort of *bullcrap* is quite popular here in a Tory seat, especially around November," she said. "When we remember the fallen."

She put the drink on a coaster and slid it over. "There you go. Your total's £14.99," she said, and Ramona dug for her purse.

"Still cheaper than London."

"Hah, I guess," said the young lady. "Much less exciting, though."

Ramona took her card out. Probably why the ghost story was so popular. Easy to entertain someone. In London, this place would have been scoped out by YouTubers and what have you.

The familiar beep told her the payment had gone through, and she received her receipt. "Right. That'll be up soon. Enjoy."

"Thanks." Ramona awkwardly slid off the bar stool, trying to make sure it didn't fall over and sighed as she walked back. It seemed she'd missed Brendon, Kayla, and Valiant heading up to the bar, leaving her with George.

"I'm sorry," George said, and Ramona had to admit she hadn't expected that.

"I suppose it is just kind of exciting to me to live in a house that is supposedly haunted," she said with a half-shrug, this one much less defiant than her earlier one. An admission, more so than a defense.

"I suppose." Ramona cleared her throat.

"You're probably quite done with all of this haunting crap."

"I don't know, George. I saw something, and it... it frustrates me that we have no idea what it is. There's... You're right. There's something in the house, whether that's Adam Lockhart or a random weirdo who's decided to live in the walls. There's that sense of something unfinished."

George looked at her pensively, and she could tell the other woman knew what she was talking about. The silence between them was intense, and George leaned over.

"I need to tell—"

"Sup, losers?" Kayla sat back down and then went wide-eyed. "Oh, gods. I didn't mean. Losers. I meant..."

George laughed, breaking the tension, and lifted her drink to the girl. "Fair play on the dress, Kayla. It looks good on you. Now drop it, or I'm making you go home in your bloomers and blouse."

"Right. Dropping it," said Kayla. She shook her head and put her hands up.

The rest of the dinner went nicely, and they caught up. Some drinks were had.

Unfortunately, Brendon insisted on joining, as did Kayla, when it was time to go home.

The guest room was set up quickly for the drunk lolita and ouji[9]. Valiant and Ramona took care of most of it as a slightly tipsy George lugged a giant Taobao order that had come through to the house.

Valiant made up the double bed in the room with one of her Disney blankets, and Ramona lent her blow-up mattress and sleeping bag to Brendon so he could let Kayla have the bed. They joked around as they set up for the night.

It was too bad this was the smallest room in the house, Ramona thought. This would make a wonderful entertainment room. She briefly looked up to the hatch that led up to the attic. Nothing would happen. The laws of all that were, were so. It always was the way in horror movies, wasn't it? Everyone saw things but then when a stranger came in, it was all fine and normal.

So, in a way, having these two drunks here was a good sign. They would keep the weird stuff from happening. After showing them the bathroom—which was ensuite and led to George's room—she left them to it to get some sleep.

Her own buzz was wearing off as she dumped her petticoat on the floor and got undressed. She fell onto her bed, briefly hearing Valiant walking around to scoop litter boxes and clean up a little. Valiant had stayed sober as usual.

She never drank outside the house. It was too expensive, she said, and it was hard to get yourself home when drunk. Especially

---

[9] More masculine branch of the lolita fashion. Meaning "prince" (王子). Can also be called "dandy" (ダンディ) or "boy style" (ボーイスタイル).

when dressed in ridiculously pastel clothes that drew attention all around. The goths could at least count on intimidation and platform heels to scare away any idiots. She closed her eyes and smiled to herself.

It was all quiet except for the rain falling on the roof, the slow cadence luring her to sleep.
They were home.
They were safe.

And then the screaming started.

Chapter 10 - Nymph

Adam breathed in slowly. The smells were everywhere, floating upstairs with the gross human warmth the new inhabitants brought.

Gross, gross. Why were they here? This was not their home. This was his home. He had seen the cat, the little beast, had taken off with his hand.

To feel this powerless was horrible.
One of them was like him. Different from the warmbloods. He closed his eyes and slowly sat up, with the feeling of everything creaking.

She had told him it had been almost 80 years. Eighty years of being here, locked in his own house, dying slowly of the lack of food.
She had fed him small amounts. He had wanted to rail and rage against her restrictions, but he needed to slow down. He hadn't eaten in almost a century, and the feeling it brought him. It was glorious. Like seeing with both eyes after having covered one.

New smells, new smells. The new inhabitants had already brought with them a scent he could not get used to, but this just made it worse. New smells on top of new smells.

He couldn't see. Not yet. He didn't want to know what he looked like, anyway. Dead, he should have been dead.

His haunt was small, but it was warm. Warm, food being brought up. But not tonight. He could hear her voice, but there was no way he could signal his hunger to her without arousing the others.

She had told him not to venture out of the attic. To hide when people came. He cradled his injured hand close. A finger and part of the hand were missing from when he had run into the cat. The cat had taken it, but he had not wanted to harm it.
Cats were a good memory. He'd wanted one or two when he came back from the war. Dreaming up names to give them. What beds he could build for them.

The noise simmered down. The smell of alcohol joined, and there was snoring. It sounded closer than what he was used to, so *much closer*. Fear spread through his veins like ice water.

But he was hungry. Food. She had said not to come, but if he didn't eat, he would lose conscious thought again. No. If he let that happen, he would cease to exist again.

He sidled to the hatch and pushed it open a bit. If he made an effort, he could open it and jump out without extending the ladder. It would close again, but the chimney gave him access back up to the attic if necessary. This house had so many spaces and entrances, and he didn't need eyes to see them.

The sounds of snoring grew somewhat louder as he opened the hatch wider. Two sets of breathing, smelling unfamiliar. Alcohol. Sugar. But also blood. He opened the hatch wider, and the sounds remained the same—asleep. He grabbed the outside edge with his good hand and slung his body through the narrow gap. There wasn't much left of him. He knew what his body had felt like before, and this was much smaller, frailer.

Finally, he let himself drop onto the floor, catching himself on his hands and feet like a cat. His senses had improved.

Still, the low snoring sound and the soft breathing remained the same.

Do not move, she had said. *I will bring you what you need.*

But she was not here right now, and he was hungry. The thought that his senses would go again was what made him move. His hand reached from the floor and found the frame of the bed. Recently added, with smooth wood that smelled of freshly cut trees and something unfamiliar. He traced his fingers from the board to the blankets.

They had to be rich. He'd never felt anything softer than the fabrics here. Softly, he stepped forward.

But then there was another noise. A low growl, followed by a hiss. He was pretty sure it was cat for "go away, you are not welcome here". He turned towards the source of the sound. The cat had to have come through the door, so if he left that way... he could go back without any damage caused. There would be suffering through the hunger, and he did not want to think beyond that. But he would have to pass by the cat, who hopefully would not make

90

off with more of him. He slowly turned and made his way towards the sound.

"Mrm. Socks, pipe down." A voice responded to the noise of the cat, and there was a crinkle. Then a loud, ear-piercing scream.

Chapter 11 - George

George shot up as she heard the sound coming from the room connected to her own.

"Shit!" She threw off the blankets and slipped on her slippers, not even bothering with her robe.

It didn't take her long to realise what had happened. She rushed to her ensuite bathroom and opened the connecting door to the other room, seeing the scene.

Socks threw a long shadow, standing in the doorway with the light of the hall behind him. Brendon was sitting up, blinking at the sudden light coming from the bathroom, and Kayla was just staring, eyes reflecting the bright lights.

And in the middle, Adam Lockhart.

She had not prepared herself for what he would look like in the light. When she had found him, even the artificial light harmed him, so she had kept all lights in the attic off as she brought him bags of blood.

This was the first time she actually saw what a vampire, deprived of blood for nearly 80 years, looked like, and it wasn't a pretty sight.

When she had found him, he had looked like a pile of blackened bones, and that impression was now made even worse by the fact that somehow those bones were standing, moving.

White bone could be seen through skin that flaked as he moved, another reason she had told him not to move from the attic unless absolutely necessary. It was easy to tell where he had jumped down as it had left a small pile of blackened skin and fabric dust.

"Shut up!" George yelled.

Brendon reached for the light, but she held a hand up. "Better not. Trust me on this, Brendon."

Then she extended her hands towards Adam. "Adam. Can you hear me?" She knew his eyesight had not returned, but his sense of hearing and smell was acute as ever.

Adam slowly turned his body, and Brendon mercifully looked away—though only so he could throw up on the floor beside the sleeping bag.

"George. That's not a ghost," Kayla said softly, her voice trembling as she spoke.

"Yes, I am aware. You shouldn't have seen this, Kayla. I am very sorry."

"What is that?" This time, she was sobbing.

"Kayla. You're a strong woman. Though I think you and Brendon should leave." Slowly, George approached Adam and guided him towards the door, Socks running off as they came closer.

Brendon grabbed his clothes, dragging Kayla to the door with him. It seemed he didn't need to be told twice to leave. And from how fast he gathered up his clothes and things, George guessed this wasn't the first time he'd had to evacuate in the middle of the night.

Valiant gasped as she saw them come into the hallway.

"Is that the ghost?" Ramona asked, peeking out of her room.

"In a sense," George replied. "This is Adam. I am walking him downstairs so I can feed him. If you want to know what is going on, I suggest you join us. If you do not, go back to sleep. Imagine this was all a bad dream."

"Fuck that." Ramona's American tang came through as she walked down the stairs ahead of them. "I've stashed some Swiss Miss if anyone wants hot cocoa without too much fuss."

"If you can call that American stuff chocolate," said Valiant, though she followed. "Can I have the kind with marshmallows?"

George moved slowly to let her eyes get used to the light and to allow Adam to follow. Dear fuck. He looked horrid. The fact she could end up like that made her shiver.

But for now, she had to manage the situation and make sure nobody was freaking out, too much at least. She could deal with this as long as nobody was attacking her or Adam.

Once she had shuffled down to the kitchen, she reached into the refrigerator and pulled out one of the packs of blood hidden in the meal boxes. This one was billed as a sweet chilli stir fry, with a thin sliver sachet of chilli sauce on top to make it look more authentic.

The Camilla Corporation was terrific at this—they had worked out how a modern vampire might live among humans, and they listened to feedback given.

She didn't bother warming up the blood bag and handed it straight to Adam, who tore into it quite hungrily.

In the doorway, she could see Valiant, with Ramona not too far behind her.

"It's my fault," she muttered. "I didn't feed him before we left, and I should have fed him when we all came home, but then everyone was crowding around the guest room and… Well, I was too drunk."

"A vampire?" Ramona furrowed her brows. "I mean, the blood is a dead giveaway."

"Well, Ramona is abrupt but correct. This is indeed a vampire, and he's been… hiding in the house."

"In the attic." Valiant looked over.

"Mostly. He also roamed around the house," admitted George, glancing over. "He's, uh… he is, after all, the one the house is named after, so it seems unfair to lock one up in one's own attic."

"One's own attic," Ramona repeated. "Alright. Great. So, we found his remains. In the time it took to call the police, he vanished."

"That's my fault." George watched as Adam finished the blood, looking instantly better. The way he looked now, in the bright kitchen light, was still dreadful, and this was after a few days of careful feeding. She hated to think what horrors she would have seen had she dared fully turn the light on when she found him.

But it was that smell. The smell vampires feared the most—that of death, more specifically, the death of one of their own.

She sighed and glanced over to the others. "Any questions?"

"Why is there blood in the fridge?" Valiant asked. "Better yet, why are they disguised as your meal boxes? Wh— *Oooooooohhhhh…*"

Realisation dawned on her, along with some fear, leading George to deduce she had come to the correct conclusion.

"Yes. I am a vampire myself," George said.

Ramona frowned. "Bullshit! You come to daytime meets with us."

"With great reluctance and parasols."

"You go out with us during the day. How is the sun—" Valiant looked genuinely interested.

"It's English sun. It's barely sunny. With parasols, sunscreen, and specific fabrics, I can last some time in the sun," she said.

"So... what about classes?"

"Make sure they're all after four in winter." She shrugged. "You can't believe how easy that has been, to be honest."

"And you sleep late, and we think it's because of classes," laughed Valiant. "Wow. Wow."

"Wait. So, is the silver thing—" Ramona cocked her head to the side.

"It's kind of like an allergic reaction more than anything. Luckily most brand jewellery isn't silver these days."

Ramona frowned. "The Taobao order."

"What about it, dear?" George had mellowed thanks to Valiant's genuine and kind questions.

"You must have ordered that stuff three to four months ago."

Ah, that had been her mistake. But when certain shops restocked, you did not wait.

"I knew we would be here," George admitted. "My parents requested that I take care of the property and find out what happened to the supposed vampire. When around Halloween the stories came, well..." she shrugged. "I was sure I'd be asked to come and find out what happened to Adam. Frankly, I was worried I'd find a staked corpse, but it was much worse."

"Worse?" Valiant asked, then looked at Adam carefully trying to sit on a chair without breaking his hips.

"He's been starving. At some point, he must have been injured and gotten trapped in the house, so he has not eaten in about seventy or eighty years. It's likely that he was turned at war and that when he returned injured and in the process of turning into a vampire... well. It's not a good look."

There was a slow nod from Ramona. "Shit. That's a lot to take in. Should he be—"

"He should be resting," George said.

"It's his house, George. Let him do what he wants."

Ramona shook her head. "Big question. What now?"

"Well, that's simple. I nurse him back to health. We keep a lovely house from crumbling. And when we move out, he reappears in some form or another," said George. "It's rather simple, and we've done it before."

"We?" asked Ramona.

"Ah, the community. Vampire community. Like Camilla. An organisation dedicated to the integration of vampires, whether that's by feeding them meal boxes or giving them night-shift jobs."

"So, those..." She nodded to the sleeve of the box. "They... wow." Ramona sat down. "I'm going back to bed."

Valiant walked over to Adam. "Sir, I just want to apologise. My cat um..." She nodded at the partial hand. "And had I known it was yours, I would have kept it for you."

George wasn't sure how much he understood that, but Adam slowly bowed his head.

"That's very kind of you, Valiant." George was a bit touched by that. It was easy to overlook the scary-looking man, but Valiant had no fear in her heart.

Ramona nodded. "That really is nice of you. I don't think..." She shook her head. "I'm sure Socks wouldn't have gone for the hand had he known it was in... use."

Valiant laughed at that. "Fair. But now we need to figure out how to stop him from being attacked by that furry helmet."

"It won't be much longer until he has skin again," said George. "I consulted the literature. Once fed regularly, a vampire can recover in about a month."

With that, the house returned to peace once more.

Chapter 12 - George

By the time George woke up again, there was no more sign of the two sleeping over. She peeked from her bedroom to the guest room, but the sleeping bag had been folded and left on the bed.

She would need to speak to Brendon and Kayla and imprint on them the importance of their silence in the matter. There was no need for any non-vampiric third party to be involved in this. Plainly speaking, she knew there was little chance anyone would believe him, as it would be dismissed as ghost stories.

There was a smell of cooking, and she realised the liberty she had attained the night before. While she had not intended to come out as such, it was a relief she no longer had to hide or find excuses for why sunbathing was not her favourite activity.

Adam had been taken back up to the attic, the only place sun tight enough for a vampire of his frailty. There was nowhere else for him to go where he could sleep without fear of a sunbeam tearing away his meagre grip on the undeath state he currently found himself in.

In a way, this was a lucky happenstance. She had cared for young vampires before, and that experience came in quite handy. There was a definite manner of dealing with younglings, and he reacted much as expected.

That was why she guessed he had been trapped shortly after turning. All the belongings taken from the house after the auction had been late-30s clothes, mostly simple outfits and a few pairs of army uniforms. It made the theory that he had been turned on the battlefield all the more likely. It was sad to think how often it had happened, but it was a side effect of vampires becoming part of society. They got drafted into wars and were driven mad, bitey and cagey.

The vampire that bit Adam should have just finished the job, but somehow he didn't. Perhaps afraid of starting battlefield lore about vampire deaths, he had kept his victim alive, clinging to life, enough to return to his own home where he had languished. A sad fate.

She slipped out of bed and walked to the shower, bringing a cutsew dress to change in after she had washed up. There would probably still be a lot of healing. Ramona especially seemed to have taken the news hard. Valiant, whom she had expected to be the weakest, had pleasantly surprised her with her resilience and continued kindness.

She was truly a good person to think about apologising after all of that. It made her smile.

George turned on the shower and slipped in, relaxing and letting her head roll around. There would be little to worry about from Adam until nightfall, and perhaps it would be a good idea to leave a blood bag in a cool bag up there just in case he woke up with the munchies again.

"You up?" Valiant asked. "I need to use the toilet."

George checked the curtain was closed properly, then licked her lips. "Yeah, sure."

"Thanks." There was the sound of a steady stream of urine. She ducked her head under the stream of water and then felt around for the shampoo.

"Did... did you get turned? What was it like for you when you discovered vampires... were a thing?"

"I was born one, so no," George replied curtly. Though a moment later, she spoke up again. "I felt that way when I had to learn about humans. I had heard of them in fairy tales, and my family didn't have any human friends, so it wasn't until I was... twelve or so that I learned humans were real and what I needed to know about this world to remain safe."

There was a pause as Valiant flushed. Awkward.

"I bet." Valiant washed her hands quickly. "There's... a lot I wonder about."

George really did not feel like a Q and A while she was in the shower, so she pretended she hadn't heard the last bit. Valiant didn't dawdle after that.

Once she had showered and dressed, she made her way down. She felt much better and had had some time to sort out her thoughts.

"Right. Hi," Ramona said, "I made pancakes. I didn't touch your boxes, but... I suppose they're garlic-free?" Her attempt at humour made George chuckle.

"Thank you, but I'm alright." George paused. "Would... does anyone mind if I help myself to some blood?"
All the indirect sunlight and the disturbed sleep of the day before had left her more drained than she realised.
Valiant looked up from her console and shrugged. "But, uhm... can you put it in a glass or something? The bag just looks... weird and slobbery."
"Excellent point."
And she was glad the girl had raised it rather than give her weird looks about it.
"I do usually use a cup." She took out a frosted glass tankard, which kept the blood at the right temperature and kept it from clotting too fast. She poured in the contents of a sachet and then binned the bag after carefully rinsing it out. The blood would stink if she did not, and she was too careful in these things. The careful ones lived, her parents always told her. She lived by those words and always would. Often, there had been whispered parlour talk of those who had not steered clear of humans, and it would already be considered grossly dangerous of her to out herself to her friends.

But she trusted most of them. Even Ramona.
Ramona was just very... American, that was all. She had a way of expressing herself. And that way was frank and to the point.

Valiant seemed to be enthralled by the flow of blood into the mug, with a shiver.

"Still weird to see."

She shook her head. "Is Adam back in the attic?"

"Yep," said George. "He needs his sleep, and the attic is the safest place, sunlight-wise." She took a deep breath. "It's painful. Especially when you are weaker."

"Is that why you get… irritable when a meet lasts too long?" Ramona asked.

"Yep. Pubs are pretty well designed to keep sunlight out."

George sipped the mug and sighed. Nice. The liquid was so comforting and straightforward. Some spruced it up with spices, but she was a very basic vampire, really.

In the end, blood was blood. No matter how you tried to dress it up. She sipped the mug.

Valiant shook her head. "I gotta tell you, if I'd had money on who in the community was a vampire, I would have guessed Ramona. Big hair, appeared out of nowhere…"

Ramona laughed. "I wish," she said. "I'm nothing special."

Valiant made her way over to the coffee maker. "I have to ask. The fried chicken?"

"Oh, that was Adam," said George. "Not sure why. But it seems he has a knack for cooking."

Valiant thought for a second. "Before the Second World War, it was a super-rare dish for a very special occasion. So, that might have been why."

"I think he cooked it to lure in food. I mean, people," George immediately corrected herself.

"Crude, but effective," Ramona had to agree. "I'll teach him how to do Nashville-style once he gets better."

"Oh, don't. He'll get... serious about it." The vampire did seem very focused, but that might just be her current feeling about it because he was so low on energy that he had to work on one thing at a time.

"That I need to ask," Ramona said. "The blood... How?" She cleared her throat.

"It's all free range and bio if that's what you're wondering about." George grinned. "There's a vampire bar downtown. They offer free drinks and food in exchange for blood. And we test it, of course, but our rules don't need to be as strict as for blood transfusions. It's a tight system, but it works." She shrugged. "I'll take you some time if you'd like."

Valiant raised an eyebrow. "That could be interesting."

"I do not think I need to stress to you the importance of secrecy surrounding this matter," George said after finishing half a mug. "I would not want Adam to be taken from this house unwillingly, as would you, I'm sure."

Valiant nodded. "Yeah, I'm fine shutting up."

"Same," said Ramona. "I don't think anyone would believe it anyway."

"That's true." Valiant looked over briefly. "Do a lot of humans... know?"

"Not really." George shrugged.

"And we'll not tell anyone. Right, Val?" Ramona said.

"Yeah, obviously!" Valiant agreed.

"That means a lot to me. Thank you," George said with a slight bow of her head. "Of course, in return, I'll do all I can to keep you guys safe."

"Safe?" Ramona asked, but her question was cut off by the doorbell going. "Hold that thought. With both hands!" She walked over to the door to open up.

George peeked through and blinked, seeing who it was. Two police officers. Immediately, she poured the blood down the sink, chasing it with cold water, and washed her mouth before walking over.

"Morning, officers. What is the matter?" She smiled as brightly as she could. "Please, come in." She spotted the van behind them. "Ah, thank you."

Ramona was handed a piece of paper, and George craned her neck to peek.

"A warrant?" Ramona blinked.

"Yes. We determined the remains were human, so we'd like to search the rest of the house."

Chapter 13 - George

George felt like that was a punch to the gut, or perhaps it was the sunlight.

"Sure. Come in," Ramona said. "We can gather in the kitchen."

"That will do nicely, thank you," said the officer. "Please, just remain in the kitchen while we conduct the search."

And with that, they were all herded into the kitchen.

To say it worried George was an understatement.

Her fingernails were bitten short by the time the agents had finished searching the ground floor. It would take Adam all of what little wits he had right now to hide from the agents.

What if they found him? She shivered at the thought. As they sat together, making tea, she saw the others were similarly worried. After what seemed like an eternity of silence, there was a sudden yell from one of the agents.

"Detective Green. We found something!"

George closed her eyes as the detective who had been watching them darted up the stairs. A fit one he was. Probably good blood.

Focus, *focus*. She looked down at her hands, shaking her head. They'd found him. She just knew it.

A stretcher was brought into the house and carried up to the stairs. If anything was being said, she didn't hear it. There was a hum around her as she saw the stretcher come down again with a bag on it. Oh no. Hopefully, they had been careful. He was so sensitive and frail.

"Did they—" Valiant blinked and looked through the doorway.

Ramona nodded. "I think so," she said softly.

"Sir?" Valiant piped up as the detective came down, and her paleness was no act. "Did... you find something?"

"Yes. We found the body that seems to fit the remains you turned in. Very strange. Thank you so much for cooperating."

George blinked as the heavy body bag was wheeled out. She would never see her vampire friend again, and worst of all, she had been tasked with protecting him. That was no longer happening. She took a deep breath and looked away.

"Do we... get more information?" Valiant squeaked, trying to temper her emotion, before putting it to good use.

"Did someone get murdered here?" she gasped, tears appearing.

"Oh! Young lady. Not at all. The remains are quite old. If this is Adam Lockhart, it might have simply been a case of his family being too poor to bury him or hoping to send him to be buried somewhere else. Just very strange that he would end up here, but..." The man shrugged. "We found him in a casket, so we are going with natural death and getting to the bottom of this. Not to worry. You're perfectly safe."

George blinked. With her stoic nature, she never would have found this much out, and there Valiant managed quite the infodump.

The detective nodded. "We'll be in touch if there's anything." The door closed behind them.

107

George nodded silently. This had all gone so horribly wrong. And it was hard not to think it was all her fault.

Ramona poured her a fresh cup of tea and then looked over, putting a hand on her shoulder.

"Babe. We're getting him back," she said.

"What?" George blinked.

"Yeah, we can't let him be taken. What if he gets exposed to sunlight or dissected?" Ramona looked over. "I'll need to make some calls. But if we find out where he is being kept... It's not like morgues are super secure. Nobody wants to steal bodies. And you have, like, vampire powers don't you?"

"Some," George replied modestly. "But there is Camilla Corp for this sort of thing. It'll just... cost us."

"Well..." Valiant shrugged. "It's student loan day."

"Yeah. Let's do this," Ramona agreed. "He's one of us now. Who else is going to take pictures of us when we're out tripletting[10] *Milky Swan*?"

George laughed, though she was almost crying.

"Thanks, you guys," she said, her voice croaking.

---

[10] When three people wear the same or similar outfits to an event. Similar to twinning where it is done by two people.

Chapter 14 - George

There were no questions asked.

George had dialled the emergency number she had—it would be light for another few hours, so this was when to start planning any escapades to get her friend out. Her ear was beginning to buzz from the waiting-line tone as she paced around the living room.

"Code please?" It sounded at last, and George was so relieved she almost forgot to reply.

"Oh! 0319-060-100-125. Requesting back up for a non-digit... being." She had almost said vampire, which would have been the *wrongest* thing to say if their phones were tapped.

And after a dead body had been found in their house, that could very well be. It was never a problem being a bit too careful; it was when you let your guard down that things went wrong.

A sigh on the other end of the line as her number was taken down. "Location, please?"

"Surrey," she said and added her postcode.

"There is only one building address listed under that code. Is that—" "The Lockhart house?"

"Indeed," she said. That name rang a bell, it seemed. *Good.*

"There will be an agent over straight away," the voice on the other end announced. Then the line went dead.

With a sigh of relief, she turned to the two other girls. "Someone is coming to help us."

"Alright." Ramona nodded. "Gosh, we're not getting involved in some kind of cabal, are we?"

"Ah, membership is optional." George raised an eyebrow. "Oh, you were being facetious. No, you are not getting involved in any kind of coven."

"Ah, wonderful," said Valiant with a chuckle. "So... they're sending some badass vampire?"

"More like a local vampire who knows his way around and will get us the help we need. It might not be enough, still, but it's a start."

"So, what now?" Valiant asked.

"Now we wait." She sipped her tea and sighed.

George was momentarily tempted to fill the silence but then thought better of it. Especially as Valiant walked back to the kitchen to feed Socks and see to his litter.

George was trying to get back to normality after everything that had happened, letting her thoughts roam free. What if Adam had looked less dead? Would the police name them as suspects? Usually, her mind was quite reined in, yet her thoughts took a dark turn, indeed more suspicious. Draining down the hot tea, she had cupped in both hands. It most certainly was too hot, but that didn't harm her. In fact, it seemed to do her good right now.

"I'm going to bed until sundown. I think I'll need to be on my game no matter what, so it'll be good to get some more sleep. Not like I can do much."

Ramona nodded in agreement. "Get some rest, George. It'll be okay. We've got your back."

Ramona put a hand on her shoulder, and George really knew she meant it. It had been a great decision to live with her friends.

Chapter 15 - George

George woke up as someone knocked at the door. "George? Sun's down, and your phone's been ringing."

George woke up immediately, jumping up and looking around. Her phone was still in the kitchen.

Damnit. She sighed and put her dress back on, realising with some humour she hadn't even taken her head bow off.

"Right. Hi." She rubbed her face and opened up. "Thanks for waking me up. Who called?"

"Private num— oh, wait." The phone in her hand went off again, and she handed it over.

George immediately answered. "This is George speaking." She knew who it was going to be, but it still didn't prepare her for the voice on the other end.

"This is Detective Green. 0335-011-100-125."

It took her a moment to process that information. Detective Green? One half of her brain was still thinking about the detective as the enemy, the one who had taken Adam away. But then there was the identification code.

They were from the same clan.

"Hello?" the detective repeated.

"I'm here. This is George. 0319-060-100-125." A necessary exchange to verify identity. It was silent for a moment.

"I know you," he said at last with a sigh. "You need help. Was the body we took a victim of yours?"

"No," said George. "He's... He's Adam Lockhart. He's a vampire," she said at long last. "We need to get him out of police custody and back to the house. He needs regular feeding."

There was a strange static on the line, and she was starting to realise this was no standard phone line. The other had taken precautions and probably scrambled the line.

"Yes," he finally replied and sighed. "I will return him to the house," he simply said and then hung up. Secure line or not, it was probably best not to talk too much about these things over the phone.

Ramona looked over. "What was that all about?"

"Ah. Um. Our back up." She cleared her voice. "Adam will be returned to the house. I don't know much more."

She closed her eyes and put the phone down on her bed.

"So, we wait some more?"

"Yeah. Where's Valiant?"

"She has been studying for a while now. Probably should have done the same thing, but..." Ramona crossed her arms.

"This whole thing is... keeping me awake, to be honest. I've never had to think about... vampires..." She shivered and looked away.

"Don't worry your head about it. It's not got to do with you." She shook her head.

"Bullshit, babe. You're involving us all, moving us here." Ramona turned away before she could reply, but she was right. She should have moved in alone, though it would have been a lot harder to explain why and how she could rent a house like this solo.

What a fucking mess. She turned to the ensuite bathroom and washed her face, looking at her pale self in the mirror.

Of course, she had known once she hit 18 that service to the vampire community was required. Never thinking it would be in such a dramatic way, to be honest. She thought she would be called upon by the odd vampire needing help or maybe to lure humans into donating blood.

"Oh, your fucking meal packs arrived while you were asleep. I put them in the fridge," Ramona called from the door.

"Cheers," she muttered in response, trying not to scream into the towel she was patting her face dry with.

This whole thing was so above her paygrade, and worst of all, she wasn't even being paid. This was just expected from her as a dutiful daughter. She stared back at the mirror, took off her head bow and brushed her hair before putting it back on.

This look gave her so much confidence, and she was happy to look utterly ridiculous to ninety percent of the population. That was never a problem.

She finally left her room and walked downstairs, seeing Ramona in the kitchen eating some of her strangely orange mac and cheese while reading a book on cell reproduction.

"Enjoy your dinner," George said.

"Thanks." Ramona walked to the fridge and poured herself some orange juice. "Look, I don't mean to be... mean. I just... This is stressful."

"It is," she admitted. "But hopefully not much longer. None of this should have gone this badly wrong, and I'm sorry. I really am."

"Thank you, I appreciate your apology," said Ramona. "If you need back up, I'm up for another... two hours. I need to finish this fucking book." She sighed and looked over to the tome on the table. "You can't magic knowledge into my head, can you?"

"I'm afraid not," she said and shook her head. "We kind of just... drain."

Ramona laughed at that and returned to the table as the doorbell rang. "Fuck. Who's that?" It was late at night.

"Detective Green, I'm sure."

"What? How do you know?" Ramona frowned.

"Because he's the one that called me." She licked her lips. "He's the backup."

"No way. He's a vamp—No wonder he's hot." She grinned.

George couldn't help but laugh. "He does look charming." She rushed to open the door.

Detective Green sighed as she opened up and carried the body bag inside. "Right."

"Thank you! How did you...?" She frowned. This was much easier than she had expected.

"Don't ask. Needless to say, you'll be hearing a lot of rumours in town in the next few days. Don't add to them. Don't say anything." He sighed and ran a hand through his brown hair. "If you'll excuse me. I need to fake my own death."

Chapter 16 - George

George rushed to the body bag and unzipped it.

"Hey. You're back home," said George, seeing the dazed vampire slowly stirring. Hopefully, he had just slept through the whole ordeal. He looked a bit worse for wear from the jostling, but nothing too dramatic. Some blood would get him right back on track to healing again.

Valiant leaned over. "Is he okay?" she asked.

"As good as he can be, it seems. How do you even know he's still alive?" Ramona made a face, then blinked. "Oh, I think he moved."

George sighed. "Of course he did. He's still alive. Well. Undead."

Valiant blinked. "Do... What happens to vampires when they... expire?"

Ramona grinned. "Expire. What?"

"The body burns up," George said softly. "Please, get a blood bag."

Valiant nodded. "Yeah. Of course." She rushed off, and George heard the fridge open and close.

"Thank you." George took the bag and tore it open, helping Adam drink from it.

The thick blood slowly absorbed into his mouth. He was starting to look better by the moment. Valiant looked away.

"Right. He'll need to recover." George closed her eyes. She would need to repay that favour to Camilla Corp, and it would take a long time.

"Right. You guys should go to bed. It's late, and I need to get this one to the attic where he's safe," she said.

Hopefully, this was worth the effort. She helped, as much as carried, the body up and walked to the stairs.

To her surprise, Ramona walked up and helped her carry the body. She had not said a word, just heaved her shoulder under the other's arm and taken her share of the weight. Sweet, really, but George wasn't sure how to react to it. She slowly nodded over and then walked up the stairs, managing to take the body up.

It didn't take long for them to get the body into the attic and gingerly move it into the casket. He seemed to have gotten worse, the skin papery and dried out on his bones. It was dark greyish, looking horrible and thin. *How could anyone bounce back from being so starved?* she wondered. But she knew he would. Vampires always did.

As much as she cared for the man and his recovery, she was glad once the body was back in the casket and she could leave the dust and smell of the attic behind. The air up there was dry, which probably helped the vampire's body desiccate rather than grow mouldy, a much worse occurrence.

She had snapped a picture of the vampire to send to her parents so that they knew she was taking her duties seriously.

117

He has been recovered and is resting. Camilla Corp takes credit.

Yet, she would rather admit that and be thought of as less than feel too proud to use the tools at her disposal. There would be many times when she would be on her own with nobody to count on, so why not use the resources when she had them?

She glanced at Ramona and nodded gratefully.

"Yeah, whatever." Ramona turned around and walked back towards her books, packing them up to take them with her up the stairs.

Perhaps she thought of Ramona too critically. The woman was a sweet one and had helped her where needed, even if she had not always held her tongue.

But that was something she valued in friendship—the ability to be frank and honest. A vampire could spend ages in the same company, so there was little room for passive-aggressive behaviour. Vampires who did not talk would get eaten even by their closest relatives, merely because minorly annoying behaviours were exacerbated over time.

Either way, she had no idea how to express this to the woman who bustled past her, walking away quickly from her. She probably reeked of dust and would need some time in the shower to rinse off the smells.

She shook her head and walked to the fridge to grab a bag of blood for herself. It would be pretty nice to have some alone time. A pack of blood, a long shower, and some time to herself to just sort out her thoughts for when her parents replied to her text and semi-failure.

She warmed the blood in her hands and walked up the stairs, taking deep breaths and trying to relax. What a day this had been, and she worried briefly how the man had managed to get the body back without suspicion.

Then again, he had made it clear she would probably find out over the next few days, and there was little else to the story at this point. The less she knew, the better, as well.

Chapter 17 - George

Her day's sleep was fitful, disturbed. Despite the thick walls of the old house, she could hear the others go about their day, leave for classes, and return. It seemed like Valiant and Ramona had taken to carpooling—they had never left at the same time but did so now. In all of the chaos, she had scarcely checked how she would be getting to university, but she considered that a worry for the morning, reassuring herself now that that was a secondary matter. Her degree would mostly be for show anyway. Leader of the vampire clans was not something one could get a degree for, so there was always that career option.

When the sun did set, she sighed and stretched out. What a mess. She had barely slept a wink, and while vampires generally did not need much sleep to live, it was considered required for mental health.

And by Jove could she use anything that was good for her mental health right now.

She changed quickly into a simple JSK with a blouse and walked down the stairs to find some blood for Adam. Imagine how much progress he could have made if it hadn't been for those damned cops. If only she'd been able to stop the girls from handing over that hand bone to the police. Adam's hand would likely never grow back right. While she could delay nursing him back to health to retrieve the hand, she feared much worse damage would be done to his mental health, keeping him in this helpless state much longer.

She walked up the stairs again with the blood and undid the hatch to the attic. She had been as surprised as Ramona to find the body up there, to be honest, and she hoped the vampire would be up for answering questions soon. She was curious about all of this, and not just how he had ended up in a casket in his own attic but also how the war had been for vampires.

She briefly wondered if he would have used his powers given the chance. It would be so glorious to think that vampires had helped turn the tide for humans, but so far, most vampire historians agreed that most of the vampire population had fled only to return after the war. Most had been wealthy enough to do so.
"Morning," she said as she climbed into the attic. There was little light, and it all came from an old glow bulb. At least it still worked.

She opened the casket and helped Adam sit up to feed him blood. Again, the same routine, and she wondered how long it would be until he could talk again. Until he could feed his own damn self again. It was cold, and the slow gulping of blood was not a pleasant sound. Somehow it never sounded like that to her when she was drinking it.

Perhaps... she should just lure a human here. Intravenous human blood, or freshly drawn, had properties on vampires they couldn't explain, but it was agreed that the pumping of the heart, the fresh nutrients, and perhaps even the taste of adrenaline all played a part in this. There was something to it, but it had become such a luxury. Maybe Kayla. She could not stand that woman.

The way things were going, she'd be glad to graduate from university. Depression was pawing at her. It seemed her actions had made another vampire's life much harder, and her mission was not going particularly well either. Once her ward had finished the blood, she let him down again to rest. That would speed up his recovery, hopefully.

"You look pensive." Valiant was cooking dinner as she came down the stairs. It smelled warming, aromatic.
"Oh. Yeah. Tomorrow will be the first day I leave Adam since the police thing. It's hard not to worry. But I have uni after the meet."
"Need me to check in on him? I can sleep in tomorrow so I can set an alarm in the middle of the night to do something small," Valiant offered.
Her heart jumped a little.
"That... would be so sweet of you, Valiant. Would you be comfortable bringing him blood before you go to bed?"
"Around midnight? Of course," she said.
"Thanks. That should last him until I return. If all goes well, he should be able to sit up and drink on his own, but if not..."
"Straws. You know what? I've got straws. I'm not comfortable with the whole dramatically cradling a vampire, so he's welcome to my crazy straws," Valiant said quickly, her voice pitching a little.

"Honestly, I doubt he'll mind either way. Thank you. Blood's in the fridge, and you can cut or tear off a corner. Just rinse out the packaging."

She rinsed out the pack she had brought down with her and put it in the recycling.

Valiant nodded, briefly shivering. "How long until he's better?"

"Honestly, I have no idea. I've never seen a vampire this malnourished," George had to admit. It was hard to see, so if the other woman could take a simple feeding over from her, that would make a difference by the time she saw him next. These small things added up, and he would look better if he didn't do anything stupid like run off.

"Alright." She took a deep breath. "I hope he gets better soon. It's sad to see anyone in such a state."

"That's true." George nodded. "Thank you. I mean it. It's so sweet you want to help out."

"That's alright. As long as I don't need to put my neck into his mouth," she joked, but her smile was shaky.

"I promise you won't have to put your neck in his mouth. Pinkie promise even," George quipped and looked away to look for her purse. "Alright, I must head out for uni. Just any pack from the fridge will do him. Don't worry."

She heaved her backpack on and headed towards the door before pausing.

"Are there any buses out here?"

Chapter 18 - George

"I can't fucking believe it."

George licked her lips and looked down at her glass of tap water. It seemed she had given up long before Valiant, who still perked up every time the door to the tearoom opened.

They had booked a table for ten after six people marked themselves as going and two as maybe. And then themselves, of course.

But nobody had shown up to the meet they had organised. At least Ramona had an excuse—she really had to study for her exams.

Valiant sighed and sagged lower into her seat.

"It's been an hour. I think we should put the poor staff out of their misery and let them bring out the afternoon tea. I can't drink another pot of tea without food."

"Yeah..." sighed George, waving at the staff before checking her phone. "THAT BI—" She took a deep breath.

Valiant sat up straight. "What? What happened?"

"Kayla organised a meet. She booked out the cat café in central," she said. To get into the new cat café had been... damn near impossible. So, of course, everyone would flock to a booked-out cat café! Her old-timey, vintage tea-room meet could not compete with that.

"She—But she marked herself as going for this meet!" gasped Valiant.

"This. This is war," she said, looking up as the tea was poured. "Ah, thank you."

A dainty tower of sweets and sandwiches followed.

"Well. Since I don't really..." sighed George, sitting back.

"Well, good, 'cause I'm starving after waiting this long." Valiant gathered the sandwiches onto her plate.

Brendon rushed in. "Trains were a mess. I'm so sorry I'm this late."

"Still not the latest I've ever known anyone to arrive at a meet." George smiled and looked over gracefully. "Good to see you, Brendon."

Valiant waved. "Hi! I'd come to hug you, but I'm too busy stuffing my face."

Brendon laughed. "All good."

George looked over, wondering if she should ask the question. Was the cat hair on his doublet from his own cat or from a treacherous cat café? She shook her head. It didn't matter.

"How was your week?" Brendon asked, sneaking a small cake from the tray before greeting the waitress and ordering some lemon and ginger tea.

"Shall I bring out the second tea platter? We uh, prepared five..."

Brendon nodded. "Yes, please," he said. "It would be horrible letting that go to waste."

"Oh, don't worry," Valiant piped up. "They provide takeaway boxes, and I'm not leaving empty-handed."

"Classy, Val, really." Brendon laughed. He'd just had a haircut, his sandy hair a lot more normie than usual. George tried to think of the last time she had seen Brendon in anything non-ouji. Nothing came to mind. He seemed to just exist in blouses, short pants, cravats, and vests. Today was more punk—a pointy collared shirt, a vest with patches and badges, a belted pair of shorts and black and white high socks that covered his knees and stompy boots. She knew he had a day job in an office somewhere, but honestly, that side of him seemed to exist in an alternate reality. She had fancied him for a bit, but they were much better off as friends.

The second tower of sweets and sandwiches came, and she smiled a little.

"Well, I'm glad you made it. I can't believe Kayla organised a competing meet."

"You did give her the worst fright of her life. And mine." Brendon shrugged.

"We warned the house was haunted." George shrugged. "If she saw a ghost…"

"Bullshit. You know we saw a ghost." Brendon tensed a bit, then relaxed.

"Did you see the new Baby, the Stars Shine Bright release? It'll be a bloodbath." Brendon chose to go for a different topic. "I'm hoping to get the top hat. If I can catch the skirt, I'm making it into a pair of pants."

Val smiled, seemingly glad the awkward topic had passed.

"I'll let you know when it goes up. I do warn you; you'll have to be awake for three am or so."

"Ugh. Not sure I like it that much," he sighed. "Fine. I can set an alarm."

"Looking this good comes at a cost, my dear." George smiled.

"Maybe I should just start living on Japan time..." Valiant pondered. "Would make Angelic Pretty releases so much easier."

"You mean those bloodbaths?" George shook her head. "Yeah, you can have those."

"That's how you get the new releases." Brendon shrugged.

In the end, they had a good time, even if it wasn't how George had imagined the first meet she had ever organised—even if Valiant had helped her. It certainly stung.

Valiant attacked one of the miniature cakes. "Don't you have uni after this meet?"

"Yes, I should go soon." George finished her tea and then dabbed at her mouth. "Everything is paid for, so just... enjoy, I suppose."

Booking this place had set her back a fair bit, but she could afford the rare splurge like this. At this point, she would just take it on the chin and keep her head up.

"Thanks for inviting me." Brendon got up and gave her a hug. "I'll see you soon. Make-up meet!"

"Yes, we should do something at our house." Valiant nodded and got up to hug him as well.

"Just don't invite the ghost," Brendon quipped.

George had made her way to uni and sighed as she settled in the auditorium. Luckily, most of her fellow students were used to seeing her in her gothic lolita garb. She was wearing an embroidered black JSK from a brand that had long ago vanished, along with a long-sleeved and high-necked blouse and heels. Her hair was adorned with a lacy headband that had a few fake black roses stitched onto it. Not really over the top, but pretty out there for a university where most students looked like they had just rolled out of bed.

The lecture was pretty much like any lecture. The professor started his talk and got really into it, and time seemed to go by faster than usual as she scrambled to take notes and not lose track of the lecture.

She frowned as she received a text from an unknown number.

> 0319-060-100-125
> Your assistance is required. Remain at location and await instructions.

Oh, shit. This was Camilla Corp business. Her identification number had been used.

> Will comply.

She simply sent back, making sure they knew she had received the message and intended to do what needed to be done. What could it be they needed from her? Then again, Camilla Corp could ask for anything from retrieving a blood bag from a vampire bar to retrieving bodies from police custody. But it came at a cost.
She looked around, seeing a few of her fellow students checking their phones or looking around bored. This class had been going

on for an hour and forty-five minutes, and everyone was aching for a break.

The professor did not seem to mind or care; he was enveloped in his own lecture.

"Oh! Look at the time. Alright, everyone, take your bathroom breaks and what have you. I'll see you back here at seven."

There was some audible relief, and most scrambled up to get to the bathroom before queues could form or to head for a smoke break to help their attention spans. She herself could use some coffee, so she walked out to the cheap coffee vending machine in the hallway after packing her stuff. There was no way to tell if a text would come through, telling her to move to another part of campus, and after the favour they did her, she did not want to keep the Camilla Corp waiting.

Another text came through.

> Move to seat J14. Next to you will be John Aubrey. He is a young vampire who needs to be taken to the local Star's after your lecture. Introduce him and remind him of proper etiquette, of course.

She sighed in relief. It would be easy to help a young vampire to a Star's. Star's was the main vampire bar available for vampires on the move, and it had a limited front for humans who could donate blood in return for freebies. Much of the blood was donated to hospitals, which was advertised. They just didn't mention unsuitable blood for humans would be used for vampiric consumption. Star's made its money from selling blood that was second best only to feeding live. The blood was usually so fresh, some said they could still taste the heartbeat.

The machine whirred and served her a coffee. She thought for a moment, ordered a hot chocolate, and then walked into the auditorium, taking her place next to a pale youngster.

"John Aubrey?" She put the hot chocolate down. The young man looked hungry and looked at her quizzically.

"Drink it. Hot chocolate isn't quite the real thing, but it'll fool you long enough, especially with this."

She poured some blood from her emergency flask into her own cup and then his, getting some smirks from people observing them from afar, to whom it looked like two students spiking their drinks to survive a late-night class. She winked and then quickly put the flask away before they could approach to ask some.

John Aubrey secured the lid and drank some of the blood-spiked hot chocolate.

"Thank you. Yes, John Aubrey. I go by Aubrey."

"George," she simply replied. "Don't ask. But a boy's name is quite good to have in this world." She sipped her own coffee. An acquired taste, but she could swear the caffeine helped. Even if most vampires agreed that was a placebo effect.

"So, you've been sent by the CC?"

"Yep, and I'm taking you to Star's. You can get delivery set up to your dorm. I'm surprised you moved here without arranging all this."

"Oh, I had to change plans last minute. I was going to live close to my clan, but that fell through." Aubrey shrugged. He didn't seem especially distressed, with a calm she found hard to understand. It was quite the effort to move like that, and his nonchalance and trust that things would turn out okay impressed her.

"Yeah, well, we're sorting you out tonight, daredevil," she snorted and sat back. "What language combination are you studying?"

"Latin and French. You?"

"German and English," she replied. "Welsh as elective. Because I simply hate myself."

He laughed at that. "Yeah." He looked up as the professor came back in. "I guess we'll mostly see each other at communal lectures like these."

"Yes. You're in one of the private flats?"

"Yes." He nodded and sipped the hot chocolate again.

"Wow. I'd never tried this combination, but it works. Wow. Thanks."

"You're welcome." This was how a lot of their knowledge was passed on. And he didn't look half bad. A boy who probably relied on his looks to sail through whatever life threw his way. It was a way she could never live. There needed to be order and a plan. Overreliance on support organisations became dangerous.

But the ability to just throw your own plans to the wind and do something unexpected had to be so freeing. She sighed and turned to the front of the class as the lecturer restarted as if nothing had happened.

She took out her phone and texted Valiant.

        I'll be home late tonight.

131

Not much more information she wanted to share, or could for that matter. Camilla Corp valued discretion.

"You live close by?" Aubrey whispered, and she almost jumped.

"Um. Yeah. Renting a house on the outskirts of town." She cleared her throat.

He nodded, clearly thinking the same as she. Renting a house was the best way to get privacy and not share a fridge or kitchen.

Now she couldn't wait for this lecture to end. Not so much because she wanted to show a young vampire around town, but because doing this would mean she had finished her debt to CC or at least had started towards that.

When it did finally finish, she was exhausted. She packed up and tried to let the linguistics class drain from her mind, but it would take a while. It seemed Aubrey felt the same way, however, as he finished his notes and then packed up in silence, waiting for her by the door rather than hovering around. She appreciated him giving her the space, even if it was probably because he needed it himself right now.

"Right."

By the time they were outside, she was feeling much better, almost refreshed. Probably the caffeine kicking in.

"Let's go find you a Star's." She walked towards the buses, but he chuckled.

"I've got a car. You can drive it."

She furrowed her brows. Did everyone get cars thrown at them these days? She shrugged and walked over to him.

"But only if it's a cool car, so impress me," she said, daring him a little. She liked this scraggy kid, titchy as he was. Blond hair was a rarity among vampire families, no matter how much vampire movies touted blond heroes. But when had movies ever been accurate?

He shrugged and walked her over to a small sports car.
"Oh yes. I could work with this." She grinned and walked over with him, looking over the coupe. "Keys." She held a hand up, and he threw them over.
She slipped into the car and made herself comfortable, throwing her bag into the back.
"Well, this is nice," she had to admit, reminding herself of where the nearest Star's was before starting the car. It revved beautifully, but even this left her with questions.
"Blond hair. Fancy car. Old name. You're not just a random kid, are you?" She glanced over.
"John Aubrey III. Technically a Lord. But I won't insist on that rubbish." He leaned back into the deep seat. If he minded her carelessness in throwing her bag into the back, he didn't show it.

"Did you really need someone to introduce you to the local Star's?" she asked.
"No, but I wanted to get to know the local vampire scene. And I can spare the money for the CC service." Aubrey shrugged.
She carefully manoeuvred off of the high street into what was considered the up-and-coming area. Or, as many called it, gentrification square.

Star's had a small car park, and she left the car there, getting out and looking over the wonderfully familiar location.

She had never actually visited this location, but it was similar to many others. You entered and slipped down the side door away from the humans' eyes. From a balcony overlooking the ground floor of the bar, you could look down at the humans mingling, drinking, and selling their blood while you sipped it. It was a winning combination, especially for old vampires concerned with the way things once were and, to them, should always be. For many younger vampires, this was a socialising spot. The elders' approval did not taint that, though the two groups did not tend to mingle much.

Star himself was walking around, gathering left-behind blood bags and metal tankards.

"Hello." He looked up as the two young ones entered. "Haven't seen either of you here before."

"John Aubrey III," Aubrey said. "0418-058-100-127."

A different clan and class than her own, but that bothered her little.

"Georgette Ormond-White. 0319-060-100-125." She introduced herself. Star nodded. He did not require any introduction.

"What can I get you?"

"Two pints of A, and I need to set up a delivery service," Aubrey said.

He nodded slowly. "Discreet, I suppose?"

"Yes. Very much so," said Aubrey, taking out his credit card.

"Of course. Our blood bags are disguised as meal-prep kits. Nobody questions those in this day and age." He grinned and looked over.

George agreed. "I use them myself," she said.

"You'll need to fill in a form. Disclaimers and all. While we promise to keep your preferences in mind, we will send what we have in stock. There isn't much surplus here, so don't expect pure AB negative every week. This is sustenance, not luxury."

"I have no doubt," said Aubrey, though George guessed a little more care would go into his bags than into those of the regular vampire. There couldn't be that many of them in a student town, anyway.

Star slid over a form, and he read it through before starting to fill it in. If it was the same she had filled in months ago, it was simple and straightforward, with little more revealing information than the usual kind of boilerplate forms.

As he scribbled in the information, she sipped the A he had ordered for them both. A pretentious choice—the more common blood types were usually more complex as they were from mixed humans. This A and AB pedantry primarily served to show that one could pay for a more refined mix than the average person, but she wouldn't fight it if he wanted to treat her for dragging him here.

Even if one did not prefer lobster over burgers, that didn't mean one wouldn't eat a lobster when it was offered for free.

She sat back and stretched out, looking at her watch. Eight pm. Perhaps she should ask Valiant to feed the vampire now, but she wanted to minimise the number of times she went up there. Adam was good, but the sight of a pulsating vein when he was starving was perhaps not the best for him.

She texted Valiant.

> All good at home?

A reply came quickly.

> Yeah. No noise from upstairs, if that's
> what you're wondering. I'm guessing he's
> asleep.

That was a relief.

> Thank you. I should be home soon. If I'm
> not home by midnight, please feed him.

A bunch of emojis was sent back. She peered at them but suspected they were a form of confirmation.

She shrugged and put the phone away just as Aubrey was putting his credit card details onto paper. All of this had to be done in person. No computers, just in case. It meant every Star's only had information from local vampires in its regional branches to avoid anyone having too clear of an idea of where they all lived.

Not that they had ever been rounded up, but they all knew how easily humans could turn against another group and how efficient they got once you convinced them a specific group was the problem.

"There, done." The pen dropping to the counter pulled her out of her pessimistic revelry. "Thank you, and I look forward to your wares." He sipped his own tankard and sighed, clearly relieved.

"How long did you go without?"

"Three days. I've been without longer, but it was in a more... rural area."

Less likely to draw attention if something or someone vanished.

"Hm..." she simply said and refilled her hip flask with the remainder of the A blood. Nice to have some for the way back. "I highly recommend a hip flask. They're excellent for storing extra blood."

"And fit well under petticoats, I presume." He grinned and looked over. "Nice outfit."

"Thanks," she simply said, focusing on pouring the blood in without spilling anything. Haste makes waste and all that. Part of her hoped he wouldn't ask more than that. It was always awkward to explain her choice of dress to people outside of the fashion.

Luckily, he seemed to get her vibe and sipped from his blood. He was handsome, and she had thought so before she had found out he was old money.

She took out her phone and checked it, glad to see there were no further calls or texts from the CC. With a sigh, she replaced the device and went back to her blood. Around her, people laughed and chatted with the smell of blood circulating.

Suddenly she spotted a familiar face. Huh.

It was hard to miss Bettina. The mint-green bob was visible even in the darker vampire pub. She was picking out something on the vampire menu, wearing a cute mint Metamorphose JSK with a white blouse. Her arms were covered in frilly-tiered sleeves, and she wore cute mint tea parties. She definitely stood out among the vampires here, but she looked confident enough that George could tell she hadn't walked in for directions.

Bettina blinked and glanced over, nodding politely.

George nodded back with a little smile as Star set down a glass of blood and a bottle of the same in front of her. She sipped the mug, then took the bottle, putting it away into her ita bag in the shape of an ice cream. That thing had to be heavy just from the pins. They exchanged a knowing nod.

"So, neurolinguistics is a bit shit, huh?" Aubrey said with a grin, completely taking her out of the moment.

"Oh, totally," she said, barely pausing. It was such an annoying course, but it was mandatory, and she knew she had to pass it to keep up her honours.

After a few moments of silence, she finished her blood.

"I have to get home," she decided. There was enough homework to be done, and she had no intention of wasting more time with the handsome boy. Deadly distractions were kind of her species' thing, so she knew what to look out for. They lived off of corrupting each other, so she was ready to hiss at him until he submitted and took her home.

Surprisingly, it didn't even take a single glare in his direction.

"Yeah, of course." He paid for their drinks and the first few orders to his address before getting up from his seat. He glanced over to the window, looking out at the humans below, sipping drinks and enjoying themselves.

"It's strange, isn't it? To be above them all."

He briefly turned towards her but didn't burden her with having to think up a reply, simply walking to the door and opening it for her.

"Thank you," she replied and walked into the cold. It was kind of nice to have been out on a weeknight to break the monotony. It was a lovely night with a decent boy as company. She could even imagine asking him out on a date sometime, she thought as she felt the gravel crunch under her shoes.

Chapter 19 - George

"I'm home!" George called out, looking around as she opened the door. The lounge lights were out, but the kitchen lights were on. The girls had taken to studying or socialising in the kitchen as it was a warm place, with good access to snacks and or dinner, as necessary. She sighed and walked into the kitchen.

Ramona was making... some sort of concoction of sauce and carrots. It was all the same to her; human food all looked kind of terrible. Cakes were easy to stomach; it was just the non-meat, vegetable stuff that made vampires uncomfortable. She looked in. "Knock knock."

Ramona pulled her earbuds out of her ears and grinned. "Hi!" she said and looked over.

"How was university? Valiant's gone for a run. She'll be back soon."

She checked her watch, probably a bit worried about her friend.

"It'll be fine. Unless there're big mice out there." She sat down and stretched out.

"So, did you—do a thing?" Ramona asked, turning off the music that was blaring out of the earbuds and stirring her sauce.

"I showed a vampire to the local vampire bar. A bit annoying. He wasn't bad-looking at all, though, and from a good family." She rested her head in her hands. "And it would be a good... pairing for both our families."

"That's a lot of words to say, 'I'd do him,'" said Ramona, sitting down with a bowl of her concoction after throwing it onto some pasta.

"I suppose. He is quite handsome and smart. Intelligence is an important trait in vampires. Dumb ones never live long." She looked at the clock and sighed. "Probably about time to go feed Adam. I hope he's walking again soon. It's ridiculously hard to feed him every few hours."

"I can only imagine," said Ramona, digging into her dinner. The chewing always got her. It seemed so much effort.

"I should head to bed soon. Do you need any help with the feeding or anything?"

"I can handle him, don't worry."

Ramona grinned. She yawned and went to wash out her empty bowl. "I'm going to shower and go to bed. If you're okay with me using your ensuite?" She looked over.

"Yeah, of course. It's not just mine," she said and sat up, checking the blood supplies and grabbing a bag. This was getting expensive, to be honest. She'd had to double her blood delivery, and while it was just a simple delivery, it took a lot more space in the fridge.

"Alright," Ramona said, washing up. "Go feed him first. I don't want the cold attic open when I shower."

"Fair point."

She absently tossed the blood bag in her hands, then walked over to the stairs. They seemed to creak less than before, as if the entire house was healing along with Adam. It wasn't as strange as it sounded; vampires had an impact on the energy around them. While he had been fighting to stay alive, the leftover energies in the house had probably sustained him a little longer. His home, his tomb.

What would happen once he was back to a hundred percent? Would they be asked to leave, or would he let them stay? While she had always had the idea that somehow they would be together, play the game together, that didn't mean he would go for that.

She glanced up at the hatch and then pulled it down with a deep sigh before climbing up. Perhaps she would spend some time this weekend just getting the attic nice and clean, clearing the cobwebs and dust. For now, it was best to be careful around Adam until he was back to full health.

The lid came off with a heavy push and landed on the floor with a dull clatter. She glanced down.

Adam looked marginally better but still not recognisable as anything more than a corpse. The skin was becoming slightly less grey and less patchy, more even, and in some areas, he seemed to be gaining a little weight, mainly around the cheekbones and chest. She briefly wondered what the old vampire looked like. She'd never seen pictures of him, even if they were definitely in existence when he was alive. Perhaps Valiant would be able to find some photos of the man in some kind of museum collection.

As an art history major, she had a lot more pull in these kinds of things, and the girl had already been more than helpful.

She heard the bathroom's soft noises below and then the pipes as Ramona started up the shower. The front door opened as Valiant came back in from her run. These mundane sounds brought her back to the present, and she tore a hole into the bag to feed her vampire. The blood ran thickly from the corner and into the other's mouth, but she could see the muscles work. Probably half asleep, so she continued pouring very slowly. The less he moved, the better. The casket would close as soon as he was done drinking; perhaps in a few more days of this, he would look better.

Just a few more days of this bullshit. She knew she had to be patient, but this was taking a toll on her. Her studies definitely suffered, as she had barely put any time into doing any studying. She could get away with maybe one more week of this before she had to start catching up.

As she pondered, suddenly, there was a movement from the casket.
He was trying to sit up.
"Oh no, you don't. Lie down," she huffed.
"Danger coming," he whispered, and his voice made her shiver. It came from deep, far away.
Painful to hear, but the warning gave her pause.
"Danger?" she repeated. This time, he actually did what she said and lay down.

He had fallen silent, but the warning still reverberated in her mind. *Danger.* Briefly, she glanced around the attic to see if there was something here that could have spooked him so badly, but there was nothing. She took a few deep breaths to calm down her anxiety, but there was nothing but dust in the air. Perhaps she shouldn't leave him alone too long.

The only noise in the house seemed to be the creaking as she descended the stairs. Right now, she would be unable to focus, so she gathered her cleaning supplies and started bringing them up to the attic.

She realised that she could have tried to get to sleep or study, but for some reason, she wanted to stay close to Adam. She started with a simple sweep of the attic, then went on with a deep clean to clean the wood and get the smells out. It looked and smelled a lot better once she was done, and she figured it could be used for Adam's room if he didn't want to take the guest room below them. Then again, he probably was tired of being cooped up.

Exhausted from the cleaning, she sat down and looked over at the roughly hewn casket. The man's home for the last who knew how long. It was very likely he just wanted out and to get on with life from here on out.

But the ominous warning returned no matter what she tried. What had he meant? She licked her lips and tried to clear her head, focusing on clearing all the cobwebs around her. Nothing seemed to work.

At long last, she walked back over to the casket and pushed the lid off, but the vampire had long since gone back to sleep. Maybe he was dead. Perhaps she had hallucinated all of this, and there was nothing to fear from anything outside of her own mind.

Gods, she hoped so. As she cleaned, her mind cleared as well. The slow and rhythmic thump of the broom, slow, deliberate sweeping. It lulled her until she fell asleep where she was.

George woke up in the attic, stirring as something seemed to change in her surroundings. Perhaps a vibe. No, it seemed to be simply the vibrations of the household. People were waking up.

A discarded blood bag had been left in the rubbish bag she'd used to gather anything left over. So, Valiant had stuck to her promise, coming up here to feed the vampire even though that was not something she'd had to.

With a yawn, she pushed the lid off of the casket and was glad to note that Adam was looking much better. It seemed the enforced rest and extra feeding had done him a lot of good.

Slowly, he turned his head and opened his eyes. His skin was starting to gain colour, though he was still unsightly pale and thin. It would take a day or so before she would let him walk out of here again.

"Good morning, sleeping beauty." She grinned and sat down next to him. "Valiant came to feed you, huh?"

He nodded, but then there was the sudden bang of the hatch being forced open. It was Ramona, as evident from her usual brash manner.

"There you are!" she gasped, but it was mostly out of relief. "We need a house meeting. Please, come down." She threw a few blood bags up with her, but her look made it clear she did not want to talk about it right now.

"I was not planning on spending my day here. Or my night," George yawned.

Grumpily, Adam moved the casket lid back on top of himself.

"Right, let's go."

She grabbed the plastic blood bag, intending to clean it when she got to the kitchen.

"You best leave that here," Ramona said with a glance at the bag.

"We have visitors?" George frowned.

"The landlord…"

"The landlord is supposed to give 24 hours advance notice before visiting. Did I miss something?" she asked and looked around.

"Will you let me finish at long last?" huffed Ramona. "No, it's not the landlord. It's worse. The landlord's sending a team of investigators to check the house for paranormal activity."

"Uh. What?" The usually verbose George was lost for words.

"There's… I'm going to let them explain. They want to do their whole spiel while we're there, so I'd say let them wait and get changed." Ramona seemed equally piqued at this intrusion.

"Thank you." George put the blood bag back in the rubbish, then walked down the stairs, closing the hatch before slipping through to her room via the ensuite.

146

"I should go goth, shouldn't I?" She chuckled, looking at her collection, before settling on a demure Victorian Maiden floral print with a high-necked blouse, over-the-knee stockings, and a simple lace headband before putting on her slippers in the form of cute fluffy bats with tiny wings on the sides.

"Looking the part." Ramona fixed her bangs, then nodded. "We're going to be on YouTube, it seems."

"Ugh." She shook her head.

The lounge was taken up by three men and one woman.

The shorter one with some chub on him introduced himself as Phil. He was clearly the oldest, wearing a trilby and a bomber jacket. A strange combination.

Phil smiled. "Good to have you all here! Let me just make my introductions. We are the creators of the YouTube channel Spooky Surrey. The shy fellow in the back is Vincent, and he's a medium. The one with the camera is Patrick. And then we have Hannah, who's going to be our host and narrator. I'm Phil; I'm the director." He nodded. "And you..." He spread his hands out towards them.

George couldn't help but roll her eyes.

"Georgette." She didn't offer last names, as they did not seem to bother with that either. "George to my friends."

"That's a great name, very memorable, and I'm sure we'll be fast friends soon, Georg... ette," he added as she glared at him.

"I'm Valiant." Valiant waved. She'd clearly been studying, wearing a simple skirt and cutsew with some thick frumpy socks to keep her legs warm.

147

"Ramona," Ramona introduced herself, looking unsure about all of this. She didn't like it; that much was certain, at least.

"Wonderful. So, your landlord has given us permission to film here after some suspicious activity. You all know the Halloween story, of course. And then there's detective Green's mysterious... death."

"What?" Valiant went wide-eyed.

"Ah, yes. The detective drove his car off the bridge after stealing a body found in this house, claiming it was a demon that had to be removed from the town. We dare say the demon got to him," he sighed and looked around. "Terrible way to go."

"Yeah, I'll fucking say," Ramona said. "So, what's that got to do with—oh right."

She closed her eyes.

"This is the haunted house," she said, rubbing her temples.

Valiant licked her lips. "I feel so bad for him..."

George would have given everything in that moment to tell her friend the detective was okay. He had to have faked his own death to get away with the theft of the body. Interfering with a dead body was a crime, after all, even if it wasn't completely dead yet.

"So, yes, we'll be using Patrick to sense any energies around the house, contact them if they are willing..."

Ramona raised an eyebrow. "Uh-huh. There's nothing here. It's just all ridiculous coincidence and hearsay."

"A sceptic! That's great. That's always good to have in the group. Please keep venting your doubts while we film." Hannah put her hands together.

George had to admit she had an excellent presenter voice.

"What if we'd rather not be filmed?" asked Valiant. "I mean, gee whizz, I'm just a student! I spend most of my time sitting around in my pyjamas, studying or playing video games. I'd rather not see myself on YouTube."

"That's understandable. The landlord offers to put you up in a hotel outside of town if you don't consent to filming."

Valiant's eyes bulged. "Outside of town? How will I get to uni?"

"Well, you have a car outside, don't you?" Hannah smiled gently. "I'm sure it won't be a problem."

"This is bullshit," Ramona said. "We either let you guys run around our house with cameras and new-age bull, or we get put in a hotel miles away from uni?" She shook her head. "And without as much as a by your leave!"

"Nice." Valiant grinned at the British idiom.

"I thought I'd give it a go," said Ramona before looking back at Hannah, who wasn't nearly as taken aback as she should be.

"Well, yes. Them's the breaks. Isn't that American?" She looked over. "For a week or two, you put up with us, and the landlord guarantees a full refund of your deposit." She took out a slip of paper promising as much. "It was apparently quite a lot."

Ramona groaned. George knew it had been a lot of money for her. And to get it back in full without any deductions would be amazing. Valiant wouldn't care about the money much, but she would be loyal to her friends. So, if Ramona stayed, Valiant stayed. George knew that much.

What about herself? George was never going to leave. There was no chance with the vampire in the attic, but she had kept quiet to let the others have their doubts and discussions. Had she said up front she would be staying, it could have raised suspicion as well.

"I'm staying, then," Ramona finally said, looking around at the other two.

Valiant nodded. "As well. As long as our rooms are off limits. Privacy, you know, and a place to study."

Smart. George knew none of them ever studied in their rooms; they were too small. But it was a start towards discussing what areas were off limits.

"Can't do it. It's part of the house," said Phil, looking from Hannah to the other girls.

"Look, we're students. We need some place to study." Ramona frowned.

"Alright. We'll limit filming of the rooms and only do it when you're not around."

"*Ewww...*" George said. "I'm sorry, if you're going to be filming in my room, I'd rather be present."

"Fine!" Hannah barked at last. "Free rein downstairs and any basements. Limited, on-demand access to the upper floors and the attic."

George froze. How did she know about the attic? Still, she couldn't tip her hand now.

"I think we can work with that," said Ramona, at last, presenting herself as the leader of the group. "We want a few hours' warning before room filming, and we're allowed to say no or postpone, like when we need to go to class."

Hannah took a deep breath.

"Deal," she said finally. "Those terms are agreeable. You can read and sign the contracts in a bit. We'll need to get them amended."

"Thank you." Ramona smiled and looked over. "That's very much agreeable," she parroted the woman's vocab, much to Valiant's delight.

Phil shook his head and just got his laptop out. "What's the Wi-Fi? I'll need to use your printer for the amended contracts."

Valiant chuckled. "I'll put in the password." She was the techy one among them.

"Wait, our printer? You better pay for it then." George raised an eyebrow.

"Right," Hannah said at last. "We want to do a quick tour of the house, get an idea of the layout. What the angles are and stuff like that. Vince will need to have a look for himself, do some test footage..."

She nodded to the cameraman, who merely nodded at them. So far, the rest of the crew had remained quite silent.

George sighed. "I'm fine with that. Do what you need to do, I guess."

She stood up, walking to the fridge before pausing. She couldn't feed in front of strangers.

"How about I give you the tour?" Ramona jumped up, seemingly picking up on the vibe. "We'll start in the kitchen as I guess it's the least interesting."

"Well, it's where our supposed demon cooked fried chicken, right?"

"Yes, I suppose." Ramona blinked. "Alright, come along."

She ushered them through to the kitchen, where Patrick and Vince had a good look around.

Patrick did all the things George imagined a medium would do. Waving hands, going wide-eyed, mumbling about energies. He had a quick scout around, shivering near the stove. But that could just be because he knew about the fried chicken, so there was a good chance he was just playing it up for the atmosphere.

"Anyway..." Valiant smiled. "I need to do some laundry, so can you guys move along?" She came in carrying an overloaded laundry basket, frills sticking out at odd ends, and Vince immediately seemed to get the hint, segueing into the dining room part.

Books were scattered on the table where Valiant had been studying, but they didn't seem to notice.

"Right." Valiant loaded up the machine. "That should get them out of your hair. I have one of those sharps disposal containers if you want for the bags, just so nobody peeks into it."

"How..." George frowned.

Valiant shrugged. "Ramona gets me into the bio department parties. Bio department gets into a lot of stupid parties with med school."

George grinned at that. "You are a resourceful one for an art history student," she said, stretching out. Her body needed some blood. The exhaustion was getting to her. The emotions from before she fell asleep.

Wait.

Adam's warning that something terrible was coming. She peeked past the opening to the dining room and sighed, closing the door leading out of the dining room and the other door that led into the kitchen, rushing around.

Valiant frowned. "Are you okay?"

"Yes, just hungry and..." She took a deep breath. "Adam warned me something evil was coming." Screw it; if it was overheard, she could say Adam was a friend. It was a common enough name.

"You think..." Valiant looked towards the doors.

"Honestly, I have no idea," George admitted.

She walked to the fridge with a sigh and took out a meal container, ripping the blood bag open and guzzling it down. "I've not got a great feeling about this."

"Me neither, to be honest," whispered Valiant, leaning against the counter and pulling her slouchy socks up. "If they find the attic."

"Maybe we can play it off. Launch a theory that detective Green replaced the body at night while we were all asleep. A detective would have the skills to get in and out."

"But still, we don't want him removed again," hissed Valiant. "That's how all this trouble started in the first place!"

"You don't even know the half of it," she said.

"I don't like any of this," admitted George, grabbing the bag and squeezing the last out before quickly rinsing out the bag. "How are you feeling about it? The filming?"

"You know as well as I do that filming and lolitas don't mix," she said, which made George grin.

Outside the window, something fell down. George blinked. A stick of some kind.

"Wait. Can you be filmed?" asked Valiant.

"Yes. No silver used. Which is why I can see myself in modern mirrors but not in the antique ones with silver," said George with a grin.

"Aaah. Makes life a lot easier, I'm guessing."

"Definitely," George said. "Way better. Holy wow."

She laughed at that exclamation. "Small things, huh?" The stairs croaked a bit as Ramona brought the crew down again.

"All good?" asked George.

"Yes! I can't find the reaching stick to open the attic, though. Have you guys seen it at all?" Ramona asked, her best innocent face on.

"No, I'm afraid not." George shrugged though she now knew what had fallen outside the window. Smart move.

"We can open it tomorrow," Phil said. "Not a big deal. We need to get you to sign the paperwork and all that anyway. So, plenty of time."

Patrick looked around. "Looks like the light is going anyway."

George shifted. Something about this did not sit right with her. Given a choice, she would throw them out of the house and just forget about all of this. It made her job harder.

"Thanks," Vince said. "For showing us around. Can I have some water, please?"

"Yeah, sure." Valiant nodded, getting him a glass of water and handing it over. "We've got great tap water out here. No worries," she said with a smile. None of them had found the water filter yet, so they had just enjoyed the tap water. Well. Valiant and Ramona had.

Ramona got a coke out of the fridge and smiled a little. "I'm sure you guys won't find much here, but we're getting paid, right?"

"Payment?" Phil made a face. "We can look into remuneration…"

"Where's Hannah?" asked Valiant, looking around. Patrick had trailed behind for sure. But he had come down.

"Yes, can we not have people wander around our rooms alone?" Valiant made a face. "You guys are strangers. No offence."

Hannah appeared. "None taken."

George swallowed as she saw how much more genuine the woman's smile was this time. What had she found? She cleared her throat.

"We would like to take the guest room," said Phil.

"Yes," Vincent finally spoke, his voice mellifluous. "The energy is strongest there."

"It's way too small!" Valiant chuckled. "Seriously. We can barely fit a double bed. There's a lot of space in the lounge, though," Valiant offered, playing the crew's suggestion off as a joke. That was probably the safest thing.

"True," Patrick said. "We can set up camp there."

Ramona waltzed in to get some soda, and with growing anxiety, George saw Hannah crane her neck when the fridge opened.

No way she knew. Did she? Ramona luckily closed the fridge as fast as she could.

"Also. You better get your own food. We're students, so we're not feeding you." Ramona cracked the can.

"All taken care of. As long as we can use your bathroom?" Phil smiled a little. His humorous manner seemed wholly out of sorts for a director, and it was clear that Hannah was more than just the narrator.

Maybe she was the danger Adam had warned her about.

Either way, she was not leaving this house if these people were there. They would have to drag her out if they wanted an opportunity to explore on their own. Ramona had displayed some quick thinking to keep the attic off limits for now, but that would only last them so long. Even this crew would be happy to grab a step ladder to explore the area that Patrick considered the most haunted. Or at least had vibes about. Patrick continued roaming around like a lost Roomba, closing his eyes and putting his hands out, palms down, muttering to himself. George wondered if this was meant to give his appearance some credence. She didn't buy it. Few people could sense vampires, and if he was someone who could detect them, he was missing the one right in front of him. She huffed and turned to the kettle to make some communal tea. That always seemed to work to give humans something to do.

Patrick suddenly gasped and went wide-eyed, turning towards George, looking frightened.

George made a face at him, but from this distance, she could hear his heart beating, feeling it like a bat could echolocate. It just bounced at her. She glanced at him a moment, wondering if he would act on it.

The tense moment slowly faded, and Hannah was still talking, not seeming to care that nobody was listening. Ramona had her head down in the books again, yawning. Hopefully, Adam had found the blood bags.

Valiant was just doing some dishes and nodded from time to time, though it was clear she didn't really care what was being said. The whole thing was going dreadfully, with George feeling like this was just the tide pulling back, ready to wash over them with a huge wave.

Chapter 20 – Adult

The routine was...
George.

                                            ....broken.

George.

Every few hours, she was there.

George.

He could keep her name in his head now.

She had not come back after she had greeted him that morning. Such a nice girl. He'd fallen back asleep, expecting to be woken with blood.

When that routine had formed, it was still strange, but he was too weak to complain.

He was hungry again; this time, he was strong enough to open the casket.

The lid slid off quickly, a testament to his improved strength. His skin was back, though his hand remained maimed, missing the pinkie, ring finger, and part of the palm. But it worked. It did not hurt.

He sat up and glanced around. This clarity was beautiful. The attic was clean, but he was sure that was because he had heard the young vampire run around a long time. Guarding him.

There were blood bags! He almost fell out of the casket in his hurry to reach them, toppling over the casket but catching himself with his partial hand. He eased it back and looked around. If the human girl was not here, that meant she might be in trouble. He did not want anyone to know he was there. Vampire hunters were always a danger. His sire had told him so when he had been turned, his lover for a short while.

He grabbed the bag and tore it open, not minding that he spilled some of the contents. It was absorbed by his skin just as readily as his digestive system, so it did not matter. He emptied it and looked at the remaining three. No. He had to ration; who knew how long he would be alone for? If George did not come back, this was all the blood he would have had for a while, and he still needed to heal. So, he occupied himself with taking stock of his body, looking down at his skinny form.

Once, he had been strong, tall. There had been muscle. Now there was... skin. Musculature was slow to return, but he could move. He carefully tested his range of movement.

He had been taken from here. They had uncovered his body, humans.

They had taken him from here into a car. Much faster than the ones he had known, but basically the same. Lights, so many bright lights, then cold. The cold had been a relief; at least, it had brought darkness. The bag. The car again.

The vampire who had taken him out with him and into the car, and the rough handling. He forgave the vampire. He had brought him back here to George and the others.

Yes, there were two others. He did not know them well. The short one was kind. Valiant.

The other one, an American. The same brashness and self-confidence as he had seen from the few Americans he had met. The war was over, but they must have stayed, the Americans.

They always had money. He carefully stood up as that unrelated thought reverberated in his head.

This was home. He closed his eyes and walked to the mirror that was left behind.

The cold was very noticeable, and he knew he was naked, but the sight of his thin body made his lips curl in disgust. His hair had grown back, but it was dull, matted. He needed to wash himself. He looked at the hatch and knew how to open it. It had happened more than once that the ladder had slipped and closed while he was up here, setting up the study he would have used once he had a family. A quiet place to read, play music. That dream was gone. His sire had told him so. But he was alive, and during the war, he never thought that would be possible. It was a miracle. Going home had been a dream.

A cursed miracle, but still. He shivered and walked to the hidden cupboard. A very detailed little mechanism he had installed to hide some possessions before going to war. He knew the house would be left empty but that people would find a way in.

It was still there. He pushed the sequence of knobs in the wood, and it slid open, revealing a blue sweater his mother had made him. She had spent so much money on the lovely wool.
The familiarity of the sight moved him to near tears, and he gulped a breath in.

He pulled out the old item. The mothball he had left in the drawer with it had probably stopped working long ago, but there were few holes in it. He slipped it on and took comfort in the smell and the feeling of the soft wool against his skin. He had to have more clothes here. He had left his most treasured possessions, including a pair of pants and his most delicate undergarments. Reluctantly, he took off the sweater to put on a vest top and some underpants before he tugged on his best pants, suspenders and then the woollen sweater, arranging the suspenders underneath as best he could. He was too thin for these clothes, they enveloped him, but the chill was lessening. Perhaps that had less to do with the temperature than with a return to humanity.

What else? He looked in the cupboard, but he had left little else. He had not owned that many nice things. He found some socks his sister had made—misshapen and irregular, but they would keep his feet warm all the same.

And it felt nice. The girls spoke to him as if he was human, though George's attitude had turned more towards the carer side, which he hadn't appreciated. Perhaps she had felt bad about him being taken.

It was not her fault. He looked down at his hands and chuckled, sitting down to run a hand through his hair. If the girls were in trouble, he had to help. He would have to wait until night-time and then sneak down again. When would it be night? He had no watch, no light here that told him when it would be night. The sounds of the house would tell him. He sat down on the floor and closed his eyes. Listening. Waiting. Observing.

Chapter 21 – Valiant

"You're sure he's okay?" Valiant asked Ramona, fiddling with her nails and pulling her sleeves over her hands.

"Yes. I gave him extra blood this morning," Ramona simply replied. Valiant closed her eyes.

He had looked a lot better when she had last fed him. George had been asleep next to him, and she'd just left the woman be— George tended to fall asleep wherever she did. Not one for set bedtimes and definitely not an early riser. She was much more organised herself.

She looked up as Hannah and Phil entered, chattering between them and George. George was probably their best negotiator, plus she knew what kind of space the vampire needed. She spoke all fancy as well, which helped in all sorts of manners.

George looked up, her smile immediately vanishing as soon as the other two no longer saw her.

"Everything okay?" she asked.

Ramona's trick with the stick had kept them from opening the attic, but it still meant they would go up there. Perhaps the vampire was doing better now.

"Of course," replied George. "They're going to go now and return tomorrow. What could be bad about that?"

Valiant turned to the lounge and made sure all four of them had left before sighing. "What if they left recording devices?"

Ramona walked in. "They didn't, as far as I can tell. Besides, they're not allowed to film us until we've signed for consent. It's that simple."

She shrugged and looked to the front door.

"Well. Still..." George seemed taken aback. It couldn't be easy to have the space invaded by others who didn't know who you really were. Then again, she had managed to hide quite well for years among them. She would never have guessed that her kind, erudite friend was some kind of vampire.

She would never hurt them, though; that was probably why she didn't think about it that often. Still, it was strange to consider.

"Anyway, I'm thinking up a plan," George said. "There's another vampire in town, and I can maybe ask him for help."

"Through the, uh, CC thing?" asked Valiant.

"No, on my own." George sighed.

Though, something in her tone told Valiant that was not how she was meant to do it.

"Alright." Ramona shrugged and walked to the back door to pick up the stick.

"I left Adam with some blood. I wonder how he's doing now," she said, and Valiant had to agree that she wanted to know as well.

Thinking of the vampire, she considered him a friend. Perhaps not as close a friend as the other two girls, but enough that she cared for his well-being.

George nodded. "Yes, let's go see him. Quick thinking with the stick, though, very well done."

Ramona grinned. "Thought you'd approve. It was just the fastest thing I could do to keep them from asking about the attic."

"Yeah, it worked." Valiant chuckled. "Kind of funny to see it fly by the window."

"Not much else I could think of." She shrugged and walked up the stairs. "Let's go find out if he's still there."

George was tapping away on her phone. She had briefly mentioned a boy, and it was probably him she was texting.

"You coming or what?" asked Ramona, pausing on the stairs, skirt swaying from her movement still.

Valiant nodded. "I'm in. I wanna see how he's doing!" She liked the idea of a vampire in the house. Well, two vampires. It was mysterious and dangerous. But... hazardous in a different way. The vampires had not posed a threat to them even when one of them was deadly starved, not even thinking of touching them. It was... kind of nice. He was not violent, and no matter what she tried, she could not imagine him as dangerous.

Ramona sighed and looked at her phone. "Shit. They want to come back this afternoon."

"Even more reason to check on Adam now then." Valiant frowned. "Come on."

George put her own phone away and joined. She looked slightly worried, probably because of the news that the film crew was returning.

"Let's go." George's voice was low, gravelly, and she cleared her throat.

"Right." Valiant smiled, hoping to up the energy a bit. But it only helped a bit. She started up the stairs and brushed past her friend. "Oh! The stick! I'll get it."
She walked to the door, leaving the two others behind.

The area around the house was a bit overgrown, with thick bushes near the porch and the walls. It kept the house warm, and it just looked quite lovely. She gathered her skirts as she trailed around the house, looking for the spot where the stick would have landed. Damnit. She was glad Ramona had thrown the stick to keep Adam safe, but it was such an effort to retrieve it. She looked for the kitchen window and paused when she found the bushes there.

"Need a hand?" A young man with blond hair and a colossal parasol stood behind her, wrap-around sunglasses on his face.
"Wha—" She jumped and landed in the bushes, grateful for her bloomers right now. There had been no footsteps or anything to give away his location or anyone coming her way.
"Where'd you come from?" She glanced around.
"Ah, magic." And she was sure the guy was winking behind the thick sunglasses. "Alright. Did you lose something in the bushes?" He changed the subject, and she nodded.
"Ah, yes." She nodded, glad for the assistance. "We lost a hook in here." She tried to describe what they had just been calling the stick, which really was just a wooden stick with a metal hook on its end.

"Ah. I think I see it." With a fast movement that resembled a spear shooting into the water to kill a hapless trout, he grabbed the stick and brought it out with him. "This?"

"Yes. Excuse me, who are you?" She frowned. This boy was making himself very at home already. Well, not literally, but he talked as if he was a friend of theirs.

"John Aubrey. Call me Aubrey. I'm a friend of George's," he said with a bit of a smile, though he did not extend a hand. She noticed briefly that her distance from him meant he would have to stick his hand out beyond the shade of his parasol.

"Of course. Come inside," Valiant said. She wasn't sure if he needed to be invited, but it seemed polite. "I'll let her know you're here. We're all upstairs."

She led him into the hall and then left him there to run up the stairs.

"George! There's a John Aubrey here to see you?" she asked.

George blinked. "That was fast. Yes. I texted him for help."

"Help?" Ramona threw her head back. "What? Is he going to fake his death in a spectacular manner as well?"

"Don't be daft, Ramona." Still, Valiant could tell that bothered George. She was not as playful as usual with her stabs back.

"Alright. He's inside, right?"

"Yeah, of course. I wasn't going to leave him standing in the afternoon sun."

Ramona blinked. "Wait. A vampire?"

"He knows George, and he looks like a very invested goth. I made an educated guess." Valiant shrugged.

George put her hands up. "Okay. Yes, he's a vampire. He's one of the local nobles, a very high-up vampire. I figured he might be able to help us if... money is an issue."

"I heard that." It sounded from downstairs. "Gee, if all you want me for is my money, at least let me take you out to a proper dinner."

George did something Valiant had never seen her do—blushing. She crossed her arms and looked away.

"What a jerk."

She liked him; that was clear. Ramona grinned, having picked up on the vibe.

"Shut up, both of you." George put her hands up and walked to the stairs.

"Well then, come right up, you bat-eared wanker! Geeze."

Valiant burst out laughing at the insult and looked away. "Wow!" Ramona took the stick from her. "Let's get the attic open while she flirts."

Valiant shook her head and walked to stand under the hatch.

"Alright. You got it?" she asked, looking over to Ramona, who was hooking the curved part into the loop of the latch, before pulling. The croaking of the hatch was almost as loud as the two others coming back up to join them.

Aubrey had left the parasol and overcoat behind, dressed in a simple outfit of black jeans and a long-sleeved asymmetrical top. The whole thing just screamed rich, from the well-made top to the artfully stitched jeans. Valiant had worked enough high-end retail to immediately have a few designer names spring to mind.

But it was not the showy new-money attitude but the quiet elegance of authentic, old money.

"We're just opening the attic," said Ramona, not looking up from her work pulling down the hatch. "We're almost there…" She gave it a final tug, and the hatch came loose, unfurling the ladder as she did.

"Right. And Adam is up there?" asked Aubrey, looking from Ramona to the ladder.

"Yes. Oh, I'm Ramona. This is Valiant. We're the housemates." Ramona waved, showing her dusty hands as a reason not to shake his hand. Valiant knew the other didn't care about dust on his clothes. Material possessions were almost… immaterial, if you forgave the pun, at that level of wealth.

"Right. Nice to meet you." He nodded politely.

Valiant almost shrieked as Adam swung his legs down, finding the ladder and stepping down.

"Holy shit." Ramona went wide-eyed. "Is that Adam?"

"I am." Adam nodded. "You are the ones living in my house."

George grinned and walked over. "Yes. I am Georgette Ormond-White, and this is John Aubrey and my housemates, Ramona and Valiant."

"I remember you." Adam bowed slightly to Ramona and Valiant. "You helped me. And you." He looked at George.

"No way." Aubrey smiled. "It is a pleasure to meet one as old as you."

"Old as me? What is the year?"

"2020," said George. "The Second World War ended about 75 years ago. I am sorry you could not be there to see it end."

"Seventy-five years." He looked pensive, and Valiant took him in. He was handsome in his own way, even if he was very skinny. She realised he needed more blood and rushed down to grab one of the meal packs.

"Here," said Valiant, holding out the blood bag. "You should eat."

"Thank you." He looked over at the crowd. "I am grateful for your continued care."

"You're welcome," Ramona said before George could answer, making Valiant grin ear to ear. These two had always had a tense relationship, and this would not help it.

George seemed to decide to let it slide. "You're welcome, indeed. Unfortunately, the situation is not looking great."

Ramona nodded, though she was happy to leave this part of the conversation to her friend.

"A camera crew has come to make some sort of documentary about the place. I do not know why, but the landlord agreed."

Adam nodded slowly, though there was no way he could have understood all of that. The concepts had to be too novel.

"So, there will be people here," Adam deduced.

"That's the long and short of it, yes," said George. "They are—"

"They are not a documentary crew," replied Aubrey. "Or at least, we cannot assume they are." He tapped something in on his phone.

"Essex and Greater London have had three instances of vampire hunters posing as documentary makers to try and gain information or well..." He nodded his head sideways.

"Shit. So, you mean…"

"I mean, don't assume they're here for the good food." He chuckled and looked over.

"Especially with the activity around this house. Documentary crew is a good cover for such things."

Valiant sat down briefly. "Shit."

"Yeah," said George. "And if they find out we know, this may be our last night alive or undead."

Chapter 22 - Valiant

It took only seconds for the air in the room to explode.

"I'm not getting killed because you were a little shit!" Ramona burst out. "This isn't my fight!"

"Calm down." But that was probably the worst thing George could have said. Ramona threw her hands up and muttered to herself as she walked away.

Valiant closed her eyes. "Well, then, we don't give them anything to find. They want full access to the house, so we'll need to stash Adam somewhere. Or hide, sorry." She cleared her throat, but Adam did not seem to mind either way. He was wandering around the top floor, sometimes acknowledging their conversation, sometimes not.

"Right," Ramona said, though she knew she was not the one in charge of this conversation. She had wandered back.

Valiant could see George trying to think up something. She was pacing around, trying to think of what she could do. This had to be complicated.

"What about my apartment?" She could hear Aubrey say. Of course he had an apartment.

"Is it solar-proofed?" George whispered.

"Of course." He shrugged. "Same as this, simple UV film and thick walls."

"Wait, I thought that stuff you put on the windows was to conserve heating." Ramona frowned.

"I lied. It keeps me from burning up. I was sure you wouldn't mind either way," she smirked, and it made Ramona roll her eyes.

"You could have just told us."

"I did. In the end. Now we've got other problems, I believe." George was an expert in turning it back to what she wanted to talk about.

"Yes. We should get him to your apartment. Adam, do you think you're strong enough to bat it?" George turned to the vampire.

"Wow, you guys can actually do that?" Valiant asked as Adam finished the bag of blood and handed it back to her. She shivered but held it between her thumb and forefinger.

"Yes, that's how I came here," said Aubrey.

"Explains a lot," said Valiant, grinning as Socks came to look at what all the fuss was about. The older cat had been spending a lot of time asleep, probably not too fond of the vampire.

"Hey, snookums." She grinned and walked over to the cat, petting him with her free hand.

George sighed. "Yes, if that's an option, that's the easiest way of transporting him."

"I'm right here," said a disgruntled Adam. He walked back over and sighed. "Right. Let me try this. I wasn't very good at it, to begin with, mind you," he said and walked back, taking some distance to give himself space. For a second, he seemed to just stand there, focused, before changing quickly into a bat.

Valiant couldn't help it. She squealed, holding her hands to her mouth.

"Oh gosh. I mean. Wow…" She grinned. "That's scary."

"It's not," George said, but Ramona took her hand and gave it a squeeze.

Adam changed back. "It is hard to keep the form. I am still weak." He looked exhausted, sweat pearling on his brow.

"Right. Other suggestions?" George sighed and sat down, leaning against the bannister of the stairs.

Valiant couldn't help but grin. "If they're coming back tonight, looking for vampires… why not give them more vampires than they can handle?" She smiled. "We hold a housewarming party. Vampire themed in honour of the venue and all the dumb rumours."

"It's very little time…" said Aubrey, though the slight smile on his face said he was into the idea.

"We're college students. Not much more needed than cider and some food. We can arrange that. We do the party tonight; the hunters can either stay or go, depending on whether or not they're hunters. We can just leave them hunting for whatever it is they want."

"And with a vampire theme… we'll just hand out fake fangs and shit like that." She laughed at the idea. "It's easy!"

"You are bonkers, but yes. We can do this," said George. "Hopefully, everyone's in better shape tomorrow, and we can have Adam bat out of here until the crew goes mad looking for something."

Aubrey nodded. "I would be happy to help. Though I am sure George and I need some time…"

174

George rolled her eyes. "To sleep!" she added quickly. "Don't get any ideas, any of you."

"Uh-huh." Ramona grinned. "But yes. You nightwalkers will have to be the ones to keep the party going until the crew tires out if needs be. Adam can join the effort, I'm sure."

Adam nodded. "Yes, I'm quite done being useless here," he admitted, looking over. "I will help however I can."

"Thank you," Valiant said. "It's nice to see you... As you." She smiled and looked over. He was quite a sight for sore eyes. For some reason, she had always imagined vampires as dark, broody figures. Aubrey, who was slightly younger than Adam, seemed to fit that description more than Adam, who was about 75 years older. Adam was just a nerdy boy next door who had never had a chance to grow up. And the war had done that to many young men.

She cleared her throat. "Right, Let's use my car to get supplies. Ramona, you're the social one. Get the word out."

Ramona winked. "I'm already on it!" she said. "Let's start this party at six, so we can get the dark working in our favour."

"Sounds good," George said. "We should go to sleep. Adam, you should take our guest room. We'll put in a sleeping bag for you as well, Aubrey."

"I can't join you in your room?" He smiled a little, but it was less of a joke than he intended. Valiant could tell.

"No, you can't," George simply said. "Get some sleep." She walked to her own room.

Valiant turned to Ramona. "I have nothing goth to wear!" she groaned.

"Just do that lavender Holy Lantern. It's atrocious, but it works."

"Thanks, George." She rolled her eyes as the other woman walked by her. "I'll just do a Halloween print. Gosh knows I don't wear those enough anyway."

"That's true," Ramona said. "I'll join you in Halloween print debauchery."

"Thanks!" Valiant grinned. "It'll be a great party. We can do this!"

Chapter 23 - Valiant

Valiant tried to remain positive throughout the day, but it was hard. She and Ramona had been the ones running around to sort this whole party out, and it frustrated her. People had been messaging her all day, asking for directions, when it started, and whether they could stay over. They'd decided to let people stay over as long as they brought their own sleeping bags and things and were okay with sleeping on the floor if the worst happened.

But the cider had run up her budget, there had been very little Halloween stuff in the stores, and their best efforts had them find about five pairs of fake fangs. Not exactly the best find.

She was frustrated, and Ramona fared no better. She had taken charge of buying snacks and had grabbed a few giant bags of pretzels and other things.

"Right. I think that's everything, and if I feel my phone buzz once more, I'm throwing it out the car window." She made frustrated claw hands and growled softly.

"Agreed."

Valiant rubbed her temples. "I'm quite done with this entire thing already, to be honest." She shook her head. "I just hope it works."

Ramona checked her phone. "It will. George sent me a text that the film crew will be coming later, so it'll be alright. We can keep them busy with the party."

"I just hope they're actually documentary makers and not vampire hunters."

"Me too, babe, me too. This whole thing is too ridiculous, and I have no idea if any of this will actually work out."

"We can only work for it," she said. "You know?"

"Yeah, but I'd rather have spent the time rehashing bio than doing a party at my house."

For all of her brashness and Americanness, Ramona wasn't a big partier. Neither was Valiant, which was why they got on well. She got on with George as well, but for other reasons. George was so thoughtful and intelligent and always had a well-thought-out opinion, and if not, she wouldn't comment on the matter at hand. She admired that.

"Right. I think we've got everything," Valiant said at last. She didn't think she needed to add that she would have preferred to study as well. It didn't matter right now. She had to work with what she had. And what time she had.

They were doing this for a good cause, and that was all she could say about the matter. And once the party was over, she could study the rest of the weekend and leave George to deal with the vampire crap.

Valiant put on her seatbelt and nodded at Ramona to do the same before driving off.

"I think she wants into Aubrey's pants," Ramona said, halfway home.

"Ramona!" Valiant laughed nervously. "No, I agree." She laughed and looked over. "I think so as well. Aubrey's hot. Got the blond and pale going for him."

"I mean, I'd do him." Ramona looked over.

Valiant giggled. "I really, *really* hope she gets it on with him. He'd make a cute ouji accessory."

"Yeah, but most importantly, she could unwind a little. I mean, damn. That girl is tightly wound." Ramona sat back and closed her eyes.

Valiant licked her lips and focused on the road. She really didn't want to get into it, but she hoped her friend would be happy. That was only natural, right?

She finally pulled into the driveway to see some of the lights in the house on. Had the vampires woken up already, or had the crew beaten them here? She carefully unlocked the door and peeked in. Nobody. Geeze.

"Right." She cleared her throat and walked in. She did hope this ruse worked and that the hunters would be too confused with all the idiots running around with fake fangs and capes going rawr.

She squeaked when she saw Hannah in the kitchen.

"Hi! I'm sorry, did I scare you?" She did not look very remorseful, however.

"A little bit. I thought George was taking a nap." She blinked. It would be harder for Adam and Aubrey to make an entrance now. George was in the kitchen, washing out a punch bowl.

"Hi." George waved. "They arrived early and thought it was a great idea to have a party." Her enthusiasm looked quite curbed.

"We thought it would be great to see you girls in your natural environment, and the housewarming party makes a great first part of the documentary. You know, before any hauntings start."

"They already started, though?" Valiant said and immediately realised she had said the wrong thing. But it seemed to not be noticed by Hannah.

"Sure, sure, but we just jig that stuff around a little," she said handwavey. "As they say in the business, we'll fix it in post."

Chapter 24 - Valiant

George pulled Valiant and Ramona into her room, sighing as she slammed the door.

"This is a disaster. I went to take a nap, and by the time I got back, they were here!" hissed George, hiding her face in her hands. She clearly was not dealing well with the stress of having the house invaded.

"Yeah, well, they're here. I need to put the chicken in the fridge." The groceries had been dropped, as George had pulled them into her room to talk.

"You got chicken?" George blinked.

"Yeah. The fried chicken Adam makes is apparently pretty good, so I was hoping..." She shrugged and looked towards George's ensuite that led to the vampire boys' room.

"Fine. That'll at least give him something to do. Either way, he'll need to blend in. I'll lend him my Roland; you ouji him up." George looked to Ramona, who squeed.

"I have just the outfit for the occasion!" she said, ready to take off. "How about boy toy? Him as well?" She paused for a moment, hanging onto the doorframe. It was nice to see someone so happy again, even if Valiant knew their troubles weren't over yet. It would take all of their wits to pull tonight's madness off.

"No!" She frowned. "There'll be non-lolita folk at the party. So, it's fine for him. But Adam looks like an overgrown war orphan in his clothes, so we should at least make him look a little more modern."

"That's true," Valiant had to admit. And it was a lot easier for them to dress him up in ouji than for them to dress him up in contemporary clothes designed for men.

Valiant looked over. "What if we distract the documentary crew? I mean, they're here to monitor so-called disturbances? I'm sure we can whip a few of those up."

Ramona looked over. "They might not go for it if vampire hunting is their primary goal."

"But we don't even know for sure that they are hunters," George said. "If they aren't, giving them paranormal bait means they hang around longer, and that's definitely not what anyone wants. Right?"

Ramona hesitated but then nodded. "Right," she agreed, looking from one girl to the other. "Now, excuse me. I have an ouji to give a makeover to!" She really was too happy about that.

George reached into her closet and pulled out the Roland. "There you go."

The lovely coat landed in Ramona's arms, and she oohed at it.

"The Roland," she whispered and bowed. "Hail she who can fit it."

George pushed her towards the door. "Will you get on with it, you nincompoop?"

A belly laugh exploded out of Valiant. She couldn't help it; the exchange was just too much.

"Ah, just like old times." She walked to the door to leave. "Let me know if you need anything. I'll unpack the groceries and keep an eye out downstairs," she promised and walked down the stairs.

Patrick had put the groceries on the table, away from Socks.

"Oh, hey. The cat was sniffing..."

"Of course he was," she chuckled and looked for the mischievous cat. "He's a troublemaker. Though, not completely his fault. We bought chicken." She unpacked the groceries.

He nodded and grouped the party supplies together.

"I see. He's a beautiful cat, though."

"Yes, he's my best boy. So, what are you up to here?" she asked. "Scanning for spirits?"

Patrick blinked, and she saw something dark in those eyes for a second. "No need to scan. There is definitely something here."

To her horror, the psychic looked up towards the ceiling.

She quickly sorted out the party snacks on the counter.

"Like a ghost?" she asked airily.

"No, more... malicious. Like a demon. It's become much stronger recently." She saw the man's hands shake as he tried to give himself something to do.

"Strange. Want to start hanging up some of these?" She realised he would need something to do, or he would become even more self-conscious about the shakes, especially talking to a stranger. She still mulled over the words. Recently, a third vampire joined, and Adam was finally strong enough to walk around. That had to have caused a surge in any energies the man was feeling.

It was quiet for a moment before Patrick flashed a disarming smile.

"Sure. I'm good with these." He unpacked the bunting and unfolded it. She realised he did not look much older than them—

183

maybe early twenties. He had to be talented to be recognised like this already.

"Thanks. You know how these parties get. Someone's going to get here too early, and people are just going to be trickling in." Not that she'd been at many parties.

Patrick nodded.

"Yeah, I'm not a huge fan. Vincent is more the party animal than I am," he had to admit, looking over to her briefly before, with a practised swing and throw, hooking the decoration over one of the rafters.

"Then how did you get so good at decorating?" She raised an eyebrow.

"Mostly because I have four smaller siblings, and they all have birthday parties. And Halloween parties. And... you get the picture." He nodded while rolling his eyes.

She chuckled. "Explains the bunting proficiency," she had to admit, looking over.

"Oh yeah. Bunting pro," he said, pinning up the end of the first line of bunting already. It had been nicely hung. High enough not to smack anyone in the head but not so high they'd never be able to take it down even if he was not around to help. Very nicely done. She tossed over another pack of decorations.

"There you go!" She grinned. No way she wasn't going to use his services.

Mainly because it kept him from getting nosey upstairs. Now, she just had to keep an eye on the director, Phil. Hannah was sitting in the lounge, happy to ignore them working around her. Phil seemed to be reviewing paperwork. Probably the one he wanted them to sign. The longer they could put that off, the better because it meant he could film less of them. Not to mention what their schoolmates would think about their impromptu appearance on a show like this. Sure, some would love it. Others wouldn't, but that wasn't her concern as much. The judgey professors and lecturers were more of a problem, especially when she was already in a field full of toffs, who thought their degrees meant they could boss others around.

Meanwhile, Patrick happily kept decorating. He looked like a nymph, taking nimble little jumps and smiling boyishly as he decorated, as if he was remembering his childhood decorating for other parties. It was kind of cute, she had to admit. She'd rarely been attracted to guys, but he had something about him. A youthfulness and happiness, despite whatever darkness he had inside him that allowed him to feel and see the intangible.

And you know, he had a cute as fuck butt. She grinned to herself as she looked at the derriere for a second, then focused back on making party food—little tortilla rolls with cream cheese and smoked salmon. Easy and straightforward, but it looked fancy as fuck. Considering George usually had a caterer for their bigger parties, she thought this would be a good substitute. And it was keeping her busy. As long as at least one person was downstairs, fixing up the party works, they wouldn't get too nosy about the girls upstairs, and if they did, she could say they were getting dressed up. Normies always thought it took them five hours to get changed, anyway. Might as well use it to their advantage for a change.

As if on cue, Ramona walked down the stairs and to the back door. She looked divine, with a big hairpiece and a flocked skirt on. It looked terrific on her form. Very Moitie, but with a nose.

"Too OTT?"

"Nope. Perfectly OTT." Valiant grinned, giving her a thumbs-up before turning to Patrick. "I should go change…" She put the finished rolls in the fridge so they could chill.

"Yes, I'll be upstairs," she said, this time a bit more deliberate. "Please, if you could finish decorating. It would be such a help. Where's George?" She redirected the latter question to Ramona.

"Oh, cursing her eyeliner. She'll be done soon, I'm sure. Have you figured out what you're wearing?"

"No, not yet," she groaned. "I mean, I'll find something." She walked up closer to her friend.

"Have you heard from the boys?" she asked, giving her a look. She knew that was something the other would recognise.

"Ah, yes. They'll be here soon."

"You girls having boys over? That's naughty for such a sensibly dressed bunch." Phil smiled, probably meaning it as a kind joke, but it came across completely wrong.

"Just because we wear skirts and cover our shoulders doesn't mean shit, my good man." Valiant raised an eyebrow.

Ramona looked over. "And I thought the Brits knew better than to eavesdrop on private conversations?"

Phil's blush turned into a bit more of a shameful grin. But at least he put headphones on.

"Right. Let's go smoke," said Ramona, walking outside.

"Can we leave them alone inside?" Valiant wasn't sure if she was referring to the vampires or the documentary crew.

"Sure," said Ramona, peeking in behind them. "Right. Aubrey's been trying to show Adam how to do the bat thing, so they should be right there." She groaned as there was a thunk down from the window, while behind them, a bat gracefully glided down.

Aubrey changed back moments before hitting the ground and grimaced over to Adam, who was splayed on the floor.

"It worked!" Adam gasped, pulling his head up from the ground. "I flew!"

"For just about a second before you lost your concentration. I don't think anyone heard, though." Aubrey tried to look inside the window, but they were far enough from the lounge that they were probably okay. Their faces were briefly lit up by Ramona's lighter as she lit her cigarette.

"Right. You can come in with us, and we'll pretend like we met you coming up the road." Valiant helped clear some of the dirt off Adam's pants. Ramona took a deep drag on her cig.

"Gods. At least this stuff is washable," Valiant said. He looked good in the ouji get-up, though it was pretty different. For some reason, she had gotten used to him in the simple old-fashioned clothes they had found him in, the rough cut of it giving him more bulk than the streamlined Japanese clothes. He fitted them well, with long legs, a slim waist, and a torso that wasn't much bigger. If she had to give some criticism, she had to admit that maybe, the socks were too short for him. But that was all.

"You have a cigarette for me?" Valiant looked at her friend, and Ramona happily offered her a cigarette. She didn't smoke often, but she needed one right now.

"You guys have sock glue. That is magical," Adam said, looking over himself and picking some grass off.

"Wow. Yeah, it's... pretty handy stuff." Valiant chuckled and took a drag of her cigarette. "I'm just glad you landed okay."

"Well, I wouldn't say my dignity is intact, but close enough," he agreed and plucked the last bit of grass off. "How do I look? Mirrors don't work for me..."

"Spoiler alert, they're no longer made of silver, so yes, they will work for you," chuckled Ramona. "They do for George at least, which helps when you're a fan of this fashion."

"Yes, it's very clever to dress up as Victorians." Adam smiled, looking around. "It means we won't look out of place."

Valiant blinked. "The world has changed a lot, dear. We will show you some time when it's no longer dangerous to get you out of the house."

At least he seemed to understand that they were just working to keep him safe for now, that this was not what life would be like. He would one day be able to leave the house on his own.

"The darkness isn't quite the same." Adam looked out over the town below, and he was right. The whole town was lit up, giving up every single detail in the light of the lamps and lanterns down below. "It's much bigger, as well..."

"Yeah, the town grew quite a bit," George admitted, looking over at him.

"It's a great place, though. Becoming a bit of a city." She smiled and put a hand on his shoulder. In the starlight, they saw him as he really was. A pale vampire, longing for the past.

How much of a cliche was that? Valiant sighed and finished her cigarette, turning towards the door.

"Come on. I have to feed Socks before the party starts. He'll probably be hiding in our rooms as soon as more people than this come crashing in." She grinned. Probably for the better. She did not want drunken people thinking they could manhandle her cat. At the goodbye party she had organised for her last flat, one of them had tried to do a Lion King pose with Socks, and she had unapologetically hit him over the head with a parasol until he had let go of the cat.

"Come in," Ramona said, opening the back door for them. "And don't touch the cat."

Adam mock-saluted with his partial hand.

Chapter 25 - Valiant

Valiant looked around. Vincent was eating a pre-packaged sandwich near the sink, but she wasn't too worried about him. Until she saw him gasp and clutch his chest. It seemed to last only a moment before it let up. He coughed briefly, shaky hands reaching for some water.

After that, he glanced around, noticing the two men who had walked in with them.
Oh. Shit.
Valiant breathed in deeply and tried to look relaxed, cool as a cucumber. It just wasn't happening.
Luckily Ramona sprung to the front. "Hey! Meet our friends, Adam and Aubrey. They agreed to help set up for the party."
Adam nodded. "I cook very good fried chicken, so there's that in your future." He tried a grin, but it looked off, much too tense.
"Yeah," said Phil, looking over. "Loving how you're matching the aesthetic. It's quite a nice look on all of you." He grinned and made square hand gestures at them.
"We still haven't signed paperwork that says you get to film us," said Ramona.
"Ah, that's right," agreed Phil, pouting just a little. At least he seemed to be accepting of the fact that he couldn't just break that rule.

"We should have the forms ready in an hour," Phil piped up, much too loudly due to the headphones. At Vincent's face, he took them off and repeated.

"Sorry. I mean, they're being brought out to us now. George said we couldn't use your printer, sooo…"

"Well yeah. It's our house, not your personal print shop, after all." Ramona shrugged a little. "You sort out your stuff, and we sort ours."

"Alright." Valiant clapped her hands together before it came to something much worse than words.

"We've got chicken in the fridge and a veritable fried chicken artist. Let's get this show on the road." Valiant smiled and took the boys into the kitchen, with Ramona trailing behind.

Valiant sighed.

"You okay staying downstairs? I'm going upstairs until the party starts." This tension was doing her head in, and she just wanted some peace, quiet, and maybe a violent video game. That was all!

"Sure. I'll help out." Aubrey nodded his head. "This is a nice place, by the way."

"Yeah, it sure is," said Valiant, walking towards the stairs as Aubrey showed Adam how to operate the fridge. It seemed he would need a bit of help with all the other stuff, but it was nice to see them getting on.

George stood at the top of the landing.

"How's Adam doing?" she asked, some concern in her tone. She had to be—the vampire hadn't been social with anyone in seventy years and was about to be a guest at a party. It could prove overwhelming.

"They're doing okay. Aubrey's watching Adam a little, and Ramona is downstairs as well," she sighed. "He's cooking fried chicken, but I think the medium is on to us. He had a big reaction when we came in."

She didn't understand that. The other times the man had been near George, he hadn't reacted that badly. Perhaps it was the presence of two of them, with a third not too far away?

"Aubrey has strong energies. Maybe that's what threw him off." She made a face and walked towards her room. "Are you taking some chill time then?"

"Yeah. It's all a bit much, and I just want to relax for a little bit." She rubbed her temples.

"I definitely understand," she said, looking around.

"Don't worry. I'll keep an eye out." She winked and looked over at her friend before heading to her room.

"Thanks." Valiant retreated to her room and fell onto the bed, but it wasn't long before she sat up again.

Now it was too quiet. She turned on her gaming setup and launched a game until she heard the beep of her phone. The girls' chat.

George:
    Turn up your volume.

At first, Valiant was confused. Usually, she was asked to turn it down, but, hey, if they wanted it up… She yanked the headphone cable out and turned up the sound of her game all the way. Some of the cries sounded very realistic at one point, but her game was just very immersive. She grinned, managing a headshot, and played another few rounds before noticing she had three messages.

George:
    You can turn it down again. Thank you.
George:
    You're good. Turn it down, please.
George:
    FOR FUCK'S SAKE, TURN IT DOWN!

Oops. She turned down the volume most of the way, then paused the game, walking out.

"Hey. What was that about?"

"Phil came upstairs and into my fucking room." George wiped at her mouth, and Valiant could see there was a sweep of something, redder than the lipstick she wore.

"I knocked him out, but I couldn't risk the rest of them hearing. He limped down and ran off." She sat down on Valiant's bed and sighed. "Fucker."

"What… Oh gosh! Are you okay?" She sat down by her and put an arm around her friend. "I am so so sorry! Did he—"

"No, I think he was just testing his boundaries. I texted you when I heard him creep up the stairs. I was in the bathroom, and I caught him coming into my room."

"Wow. We need to throw them out on their asses!" Valiant gasped.

"No! Actually, maybe. Come downstairs with me?" George was shaking, hiding her face a little, and she wondered what this guy had done to her exactly. Actually, she didn't want to know. This guy would be dead if she found out he had touched her.

The stairs creaked as they walked down.

"What happened? Phil ran down here with his face in his hands." A confused-looking Vince said, though it seemed he didn't take very long to put two and two together, "Did he come upstairs?"

Ramona nodded.

"He did. He came into my room while I was in my bathroom. So, that was not the arrangement, and I want you all out of here." She was fuming. It was likely she was pulling a bluff to make sure they knew what was at stake if they tried something like this again.

Patrick, still looking a little pale, nodded. "Perhaps we should go. We've been here all day without filming. You know what that means for our pay."

Hannah didn't seem to hear him, putting her hands together. "I apologise for my crew member. I swear it won't happen again."

Crew member? Wasn't Phil meant to be the head honcho of this whole thing? Valiant felt her head swim. Something didn't add up here, and she wasn't feeling at all reassured by the woman talking down to her.

"Right," Valiant said. "But we had an agreement for you to stay down the stairs, and you broke it. Phil ran off. I think you should leave too."

While, at first, she was sure they had been bluffing about seeing the crew leave, right now, she didn't feel at ease at all about the whole thing.

Hannah straightened up. "No. I'm sorry. I can't leave here just yet." She turned around to make clear that that was the end of it as far as she was concerned.
"Besides, I just have to try that famed fried chicken that has a whole village enthralled."

Chapter 26 - Valiant

Valiant felt chills run down her spine.

That simple statement told her that Hannah was well aware that Adam wasn't an average grad student coming over to help decorate the place but something way more than that. That did not sit very well with her.

"Okay…" Valiant heard herself say, her voice trembling. None of this made any sense anymore, and she just wanted to run. She glanced over to George, who let out a little growl.

It was not too late. She could still get in her car and get away from these strangers that had forced themselves into her life. Not just the film crew but also the vampires, including George.

There was a noise outside as a van took off with screeching tyres. Vincent gasped and ran out. He clearly didn't understand any of this either.

"Fuck! He took the truck!" Vincent exclaimed, yelling loudly and kicking the soft ground outside. That was their way out, so whether Phil had done that on purpose or had planned it, the crew was now kind of stuck here until other transport was arranged.

Outside, there was the noise of cars stopping, and for a blissful moment, Valiant hoped it was the fucker, back with his truck, coming to grab them to leave so that none of them would have to deal with more of this. This was draining her, and her head was swimming.

"Guess who brought the party!" Brendon made his way in with a case of boxed wine. Classy as always.
Valiant blinked until she realised. They were having a party. The mood turned quickly. Brendon had that effect on people.

Immediately, Ramona rushed over.
"Aaah! You made it!" She hugged Brendon and looked over.
"You look amazing!" Brendon looked over Ramona, twirling her.
"Oh! I came straight from my course and brought a few of the guys. Who are they?"
"Oh! They're... a documentary crew doing a thing on the history of the house. YouTubers," Valiant said, walking over to take the boxed wine. She wanted to whisper to him to leave, to just run and take her with them, but the other boys were already streaming inside alongside them.

He smelled nice. He'd foregone the ouji outfits, clearly because he had just come from class. It made him look so very different, and it contributed to her disorientation. She hugged Brendon and then let Ramona do her greeting bit.

"Daamn, bringing the classy stuff!" Ramona laughed at the wine. "This is going to be such a great party."

Valiant nodded. At least with people here, nothing could happen, right? They were just going to have a party.

Chapter 27 – Valiant

"Is that fried... chicken I smell?"

It was one of the boys in Brendon's class who hadn't bothered to introduce himself. He was the type who thought everyone knew who he was, so he probably just hadn't considered introducing himself.

"Ah! Yes! There's a story about this house, that the ghost who haunts it, or the demon, depending on whom you talk to, makes fried chicken to lure souls in," said George, making big eyes to make it seem spookier. It worked. Valiant couldn't help but laugh at it.

"So, you can see why we couldn't resist making fried chicken in this house, of course," Ramona added, though she had barely looked away from the crew. Hannah stood her ground. Vince looked a little lost, and Patrick had just crashed onto the sofa.

"So, aren't they... filming?" The dudebro ran a hand through his hair, clearly ready for his close-up.

"Oh, no, they haven't got their permission sorted. It's a situation," George said, glancing at the crew.

"Right." The dudebro looked crestfallen but at least made an effort to hide it.

"Right." Valiant smiled.

"We've got more people coming!" Brendon looked up from his phone. "Mary is definitely coming. She's always up for a party, and I had to talk her out of wearing her white Shirring Princess JSK. Imagine a glass of wine on that white treasure! Nuh-uh. She'd kill whoever spilled it. I told her to wear a dark dress or some Bodyline. She hung up on me after that." He grinned, knowing full well what he did.

"You know she wouldn't admit to the Bodyline in her closet if you tortured her. She's been trying to find a way to sell it that doesn't trace back to her, so she doesn't tarnish her brand whore cred," laughed Valiant.

Brendon nodded. "If she wears Bodyline, I will bow down to her."

"Hahaha! Shit!" Valiant looked down. "I am so underdressed. Be right back!" She jogged up the stairs. No time to coord now; she would just rely on her good old black Milky Planet OP and put some stickers on her face.

If she was going to die tonight due to insane vampire hunters, she might as well look fucking amazing.

She brushed her hair and then put it in high pigtails, teasing them up into a loose volume before putting stickers and hairclips on. In a way fearing that whatever she was not wearing could very well be left behind if they did flee the house, she grabbed all of her favourite accessories and put on her favourite cardigan—a Vivienne Westwood treasure she was not planning to leave behind.

She put on some simple low heel shoes. While really she would have preferred her rocking horse shoes, there was no way she could run in those. She could barely stand and walk in them in the house! No, they would stay behind. Still, she put them and a few of her favourite dresses in a big backpack. If she did have a few minutes before she had to run, she would grab that and get going. Her wallet was in her dress pocket, and her phone was charged. As usual, she had forgotten it in her room, but it had been on the wireless charging pad.

Right. Time to go face the music.

In a way, even if she had been planning for the worst-case scenario, it made her feel a lot better. She had taken some control back. She looked into her wardrobe and checked she hadn't left behind anything she couldn't bear to miss. All of it was replaceable—and she knew. It was just the dresses she liked, the ones she had bought from friends, the ones that had happy memories, that she had packed. That sentimental value was much bigger than anything she could ever sell the dresses for, so she was going to hold on to those things that made her happy.

She walked down the stairs, her game face on this time.

"Hi!" She grinned, and it seemed Brendon noticed the change in her.

"Daaamn girl! Looking amazing!" He looked over at her. "Wow... I hadn't seen you wear that one."

"I've been keeping it for a special occasion, I guess. So worried about ruining it." Valiant smiled, and it felt as shaky as she did.

"Nothing will happen to your dress, my sweet." Brendon smiled and squeezed her hand.

George nodded daintily. "On my life. Your dress will live through tonight and see other meets."

Valiant realised George was no longer talking about the dress, and she appreciated it so much. She always felt like the weakest, the most coddled one in the household, but she had her courage. She had taken it back into her own hands to take her destiny back in a big skirt with a giant bow on her head and stickers on her face.

"Yeah. I'm sure it will." And this time, her smile came naturally.

George nodded, smiling a little as well. She understood.

Ramona walked over. "You fucks better come join the party. I'm running out of British jokes to tell!"

"Right then, I'll bring the snacks out," said George, taking a deep breath. The warm oil was starting to spread its smell, making for a change in the household. She walked into the kitchen and took out her snacks from the fridge, the mini salmon rolls now looking paltry compared to freshly made fried chicken. To be fair, it smelled delicious, and it was amusing to see Aubrey being bossed around by Adam, who had a process for his fried chicken. There was a knock on the kitchen door.

"Fucking hell Brendon, we'll be right out. Take your make-out sessions elsewhere!" Valiant yelled. It wasn't uncommon for Brendon to pick up a girl or boy at a party, but he usually took longer.

Whoever it was seemed to hesitate from the shadows under the door, then the figure slinked away.

Valiant breathed in deeply and let out a sigh. That probably hadn't been Brendon, or he would have responded or at least tried again.

She shook her head.

Why was the YouTube crew still here? she wondered. They didn't get to film, so... They were apparently still waiting for the paperwork, but with Phil having driven off, she pondered what the heck their plan was. The thought that these guys weren't legit kept creeping up.

George and Ramona bustled into the kitchen.

"Right. Their paperwork arrived."

Ramona spread the printed pages out on the kitchen counter.

"It all looks pretty standard..." Valiant read through it as best she could. Nothing too terrible, but she didn't think vampire hunting would be mentioned in the contract.

"So, we sign? That'll only give them more reason to stay if they are hunters."

"What about that Carmilla Corporation place?" Valiant asked, remembering how reluctant George had been to call them but also how efficiently they had helped them with the problem of moving the body.

George sighed. "I would rather not. They're not our personal assassins or bodyguards. They might as well tell us to simply leave."

"Is that an option?" Ramona asked.

"Not unless you have a way to sunproof the car while still being able to drive it, it isn't," said George sombrely. "We'd have to get far away, and a few hours of driving would probably not get us far enough out. Besides, once we leave, they know exactly the spots where we would be able to shelter. We would just be sitting ducks, honestly."

Valiant shivered at that, shuddering at the thought of leaving the house. She and Ramona could leave, but she didn't want to bring it up. George needed them right now—if they left, how was she going to defend herself against possible hunters?

Again the knocking. This time it made Valiant jump, and she took a deep breath.

"I think that's our sign to get out," said Ramona. "We are the hostesses, after all. Let's sign this. They're not leaving without their footage, and not signing it won't help much either." It seemed their time to scheme had run out. Ramona put on a big smile, but Valiant could tell it was far from genuine.

Valiant looked briefly at her watch. Seven thirty pm. She was starving, and the chicken smelled great. She knew what her next stop would be.

In turn, the girls signed the paperwork.

Chapter 28 – Valiant

Whoever had knocked so insistently had taken off by the time they threw open the door to the lounge. Socks rushed in and sought solace underneath the kitchen table, and Valiant moved over to give him a bit of attention.

"I'll be right out! Just let me make sure he's okay first," she said, looking up at the two others.

Ramona nodded. "Okay, sweetie, we can put a sign on the door saying it's off-limits, so Socks can chill here," she suggested. And it meant Adam would be left alone.

"That'd be great, thanks. Just leave the door open." Socks had a litter box in the adjacent room, so to just lock him in here would be no good, either.

Ramona simply nodded and walked out with George, leaving the door ajar. The brief noise of the party crept in, then faded again as the door closed.

Valiant would have loved to stay here, just spend some time with Socks and leave the other two to deal with it. They seemed to have a much better idea of whatever plan they were doing, anyway. She grabbed her plate of snacks and walked into the party before nipping back to the kitchen to check on Socks.

Or maybe, like her, they were just winging it. Maybe they just hid it better. That thought crept in from time to time, and she tried not to dismiss it. She was not dumber or more intelligent than the other two. They had no hidden gifts; she did not.

Okay, except for George. She seemed able to turn into a bat. Or maybe that was just the boy vampires? She chuckled at the idea, looking under the table to find Socks.

"Yeah, I get you," she chuckled. "Hiding under the table sounds like more fun right now."

Hopefully, Socks would doze off. She changed tactics from tactical, concentrated scritchies to big all-over strokes, feeling the little body under her hands relax, and the breathing slow a little. Soon, he was softly snoring. Luckily, when it came to evacuating, he was a pretty easy-going cat. He'd snuck into Ramona's large purses often enough, and he could easily be picked up and carried. So, grabbing him would be a priority before even the backpack upstairs.

The noise of the party was starting to rev up, so it was pretty much time for her to go join. She also wanted some of that chicken and to figure out what this team wanted. She tried to tell herself that she would be able to tell from a single look, an exchanged glance, maybe a nod. But this was not one of her mystery novels. It was real life, and people could die.

That scared her. Either way. She left the sleeping cat and crawled from under the table.

George looked up as she emerged. "How's Socks doing with all this?"

"Oh, you know. He's already asleep." She grinned and looked around.

She took a deep breath and then walked over to the serving platter of fried chicken, filling a paper plate with a few breasts and grabbing the ketchup.

"I'm starving, and this smells amazing. Thank you, Adam."

She touched his shoulder. "I bet it'll taste amazing as well."

Adam grinned and sipped from the bloodbag he was holding as the oil heated up for a new batch.

"Thanks, Valiant, I appreciate it."

She still wasn't used to hearing him speak, but she decided it was lovely. It sounded good. His voice… suited him, and she hoped he would not have to lose it again.

"Let me know what you think of it." Adam finished the blood, tossed the blood bag, and washed his hands. Valiant noted that with the other two vampires present, George had let up on her strict washing and cleaning of the plastic pouches. Aubrey was rinsing his out and then washed his hands.

He was an unknown factor, but he had stood by their side. And if George trusted him, so would she.

"So, Aubrey, have you been a vampire long?" she asked and immediately regretted it. It probably wasn't something to ask.

"Ah, I was… adopted, let's call it that, a few years ago."

He looked over with a smile, preparing the dipping mixtures for Adam. It looked like he, too, had been given a job to keep him busy. And in the kitchen, most importantly.

207

Valiant nipped out to say hi to people and see who had arrived after she had last ventured out. The party was really getting started, and she smiled, seeing one of her favourite lolita friends. "Penny!" she called over and waved, jumping a little.

The redhead turned around, a smile in her big green eyes. "Val!" The two ran up to each other and hugged.

"I haven't seen you in forever!" Penny smiled. She wore a beautiful Haenuli op, red with short sleeves, with cute golden crowns and other royal regalia adorning the hemline. She had paired it with the matching headdress, which was helping to keep her voluminous red hair in place.

"Gosh, you look amazing! How have you been?" Valiant asked.

Penny smiled. "I've been alright. How about you? Oh! Happy new house!" she said, holding out a little present box.

"Oh, you shouldn't have!" Valiant smiled.

"Nonsense. Just a little something I made." Penny kissed her cheek. "Oh! There's George. Let me go say hi to her!"

Valiant smiled as Penny wandered off, pocketing the present for later and socialising some more. After a while, she again yearned for the peace and quiet of the kitchen and retreated.

Chapter 29 – Valiant

Adam looked over and slowly removed the chicken from the oil, letting it drip a second before placing it on the paper towels as Valiant walked back in. "This is wonderful stuff." He smiled a little, looking over as the grease was partially soaked up by the paper towels underneath.

"We didn't have these things when I…" He stopped himself and merely inclined his head.

"Well, we didn't."

Valiant nodded. "I'm surprised you know the recipe, or did you learn after…" She made a gesture, though she wasn't sure how to gesture out "after you were turned into a vampire" while grabbing a piece of hot fried chicken.

"Yes, this was a popular recipe back in the day. I suppose you must have perfected it by now," said Adam. "And go slow on that. That's hot."

"Yup, noticed, thank you. But no! It's still just chicken, breading, and frying. It's great the way you make it, though!" She smelled the piece of chicken in her hand and groaned. It smelled simply divine. Hints of paprika, pepper, and lemon.

"Well, thank you," he said, sounding touched. Probably just hadn't had that many friendly interactions in a while, so she was happy to be a positive in his life.

He seemed such a genuinely kind soul, so different from the other two vampires in the house.

She didn't know Aubrey very well, but it was clear he wouldn't be afraid to get his claws dirty if it came to that.

George, well, she was like a mother goose to her. But even the sweetest mama goose bit if you pushed her too far, and George was definitely capable of violence. While people often thought Ramona's loud and outspoken nature meant you did not want to piss her off, George's silent rage was often the real force in the household.

Aubrey finished making the punch and carefully poured it into the dispenser—something that looked like a giant mason jar with a little glass tap at the bottom.

"Why not the punch bowl? I know we have one," asked Valiant, putting the chicken down reluctantly to walk to the cupboard to help him find it. He probably hadn't seen it.

"Well, it's smaller, but it's harder to spike this way." Aubrey kept his eyes on the lemonade and booze mixture he was pouring into the receptacle.

"But it already has booze. Why would anyone want to spike it?" Valiant asked with a frown.

"With holy water, Valiant," said Aubrey. "It's a dirty trick vampire hunters use, and it's like acid to vampires. It isn't great for humans with even the least bit of demonic influence in their bloodstreams, soo, generally avoiding letting your guests drink holy water is a good decision."

"Oh. I had no idea. Is demon lineage that common?" Valiant asked. Nothing seemed to surprise her anymore.

Aubrey grinned. "Yep, more than you'd expect. But I invite you to try and have some holy water, see how you feel."

"Don't encourage that sort of thing!" George walked in with some empty platters and hit Aubrey over the head. "Is he being a dick?"

"No, uh, he's very informative." Valiant cleared her throat and went to pick up her piece of chicken, now she realised it would soon be taken out to the main party room. The brief opening of the door had already brought in a sample of the loud music being played, and she would have to make an appearance. She shivered and bit into the now cooler fried chicken.

And by Jove, it was terrific. The crisp was there, but the chicken was tender and juicy. She let out a groan of joy and looked at Adam.

"Where have you been all my life?" she asked during the few seconds her mouth was free of chicken before biting in again.

"Um, in your attic." Adam blinked, making Aubrey snort.

Aubrey shook his head. "I'll go take the booze out. How are our hunters doing?"

"I told the frat boys Hannah was a teaching assistant, so they've been hitting on her without letting up." George grinned.

"Ruthless. I like it," said Valiant before taking another bite of the chicken. "Wow!" She shook her head.

"You know they're about as toothless as they come," yawned George. She clearly had spent too much time running around already, so Valiant was reminded of the urgency of finishing this fight before the strongest people on her side needed a time-out.

Ramona walked in. "I can't find Vincent. I lost track of him," she hissed.

"Fuck. The ground floor is easy to oversee, so if he's not there, he's either in the study or upstairs," Valiant concluded. "Let me go check."

She reluctantly finished the piece of chicken and threw the bone in the compost bin.

"Not alone, you're not." Ramona put her hands on her hips. "After what that one shithead tried in George's room, I'm coming with you. We're more useful as scouts anyway."

"Agreed," said George. "Aubrey and I can hold the fort in the kitchen until you get back, so get out there and find that freckle-butted medium."

"How do you know…" Aubrey frowned, coming back in. "The punch is ready."

"Thank you, Aubrey, and don't worry your pretty head about it." George petted him on the head. It was such an intimate gesture that she immediately exchanged a glance with Ramona, who raised an eyebrow, then turned towards the door.

"Come on, time to go hunt a medium."

Chapter 30 – Valiant

First and foremost, Valiant wanted to check the study. Not only because it was on the same floor but also because the party hadn't seeped into that area yet. She didn't worry about some couple making out—Socks would be reasonably safe from those anyway. What she did worry about was someone harming him to keep him quiet.

She took three firm steps out and made a beeline for the study, not making eye contact with anyone so they wouldn't start any conversations. The last thing she wanted was to be side-tracked while on her mission, one of the few where she would be helpful.

Damn, a lot of people had come. She glanced around briefly but didn't see Patrick. Hannah looked about ready to kick a boy in the gonads, but that was fine by her. Vincent was sitting on the couch, checking the paperwork, before he jumped up and walked away. Where was that boy going? Was he going to start filming?

She gasped as she bumped into someone.
"Brendon!" She could feel the relief in her own voice and worried it would alarm the ouji. "You, uh, having a good time?" she asked. "Let's catch up soon!"

"Yeah, catch you in a bit!" he said a bit louder, then walked to the punch… dispenser. It still looked so wrong. The punch bowl would have looked much more proper.

She walked to the study and blinked. There was a ring of salt on the floor, and some red lamps were set up in a square around the salt. Patrick sat in the middle.

"I invite any spirit present here to show itself," Patrick said, and then she noticed Vincent. He was wearing some kind of Go-Pro-like setup.

"There's a definite chill in the air…" Vincent said softly. They both had their backs to her, so they were probably too caught up in… whatever this was to notice her.

"Maybe we should lay out the chicken bone," Patrick said, repeating his chant. He took out a chicken bone from a plastic container and looked around before launching into a bit of a narration.

"It was said that the ghost which haunts this place has a penchant for meat. Last October, almost a year ago, three boys came here to trick or treat. One of them tried the door, and it was ripped open by an apparition with red eyes, almost eight foot tall, with bones hanging from his cloak as if it was… collecting them. It smelled of death, the boys said, and bellowed out a demonic howl before clawing at the child. They found a plate of fried chicken not too far away. So, we're hoping the bone will draw out the ghost… Vincent, are you filming this? Don't cross the salt circle—if it's disturbed…"

"There's a gap in the circle," Patrick gasped, camera whipping around. Valiant found herself briefly in the frame before moving back.

Then there was a scream. "Did you see that?"

The bone in the circle was gone.

"Socks! Drop it. Not good for you…" Valiant sighed and crouched down to wrestle the bounty from Socks's mouth.

"Nice one. Have you caught any ghosts yet?" George grinned.

This put her much more at ease. They would not go to these lengths to film something just to convince them they weren't dangerous.

Ramona rushed in. "Everything okay here?"

"Yeah, we were trying to lure the ghost with some chicken bones…" Patrick laughed and looked over at the two of them. "I'm glad that chonk of a cat didn't eat it."

"He's not fat!" Valiant picked up Socks and gave him a cuddle. "He's just a moggy, and part of his lineage must be Maine Coon or something."

"Why are you blaming the Americans when he literally eats his own body weight if you let him?" Ramona shook her head, but she still gave the cat some scritchies on the head.

"Maybe we should go upstairs. Is there any room where the activity is quite… concentrated?"

Well, now that Adam was passing as a human… Valiant looked at Ramona, who smiled knowingly.

"Yes, apparently the attic. Let's take you up, now that you have the proper permissions," Ramona said, though Valiant knew the whole ritual had put George at ease as much as it had her.

"Though you better clean up that salt when we're done here," said Valiant.

The trip to the attic was pretty uneventful. They made their way up with George, Vincent, and Patrick in tow.

Patrick shivered as soon as he set foot in the attic.

"Oh yes. Something definitely resides here. It's... soaked through with energy." The medium licked his lips.

"Yes, the temperature here is definitely lower."

"It's an attic," Valiant said before getting a poke in the ribs from Ramona, who seemed to be enjoying this.

"Oh, there's a casket here!" Patrick walked over and opened it up. "It's empty. Whoever... or whatever... rested here must be out."

"Did you hear that?" Vincent whipped around. "Okay, I think I just saw the casket move... and..."

"Turn off your lights," Patrick said, licking his lips again and turning off his own torch.

"We're switching to night vision mode and heat vision... If anything is up here, we'll find it."

Valiant was trying not to laugh. This was brilliant. She almost wished one of the vampires was up here to scare them.

"Alright, we're going to set up the EVP... Electronic Voice Phenomenon equipment." Vincent turned the camera off.

"Okay, let's turn the lights back on."

Valiant grinned and turned the light in the attic on. It wasn't much—a lightbulb on a most basic string.

"Thanks. So, we're going to be setting up our equipment. I'm guessing one or both of you want to stay as we film?" Vincent asked.

"Sure," Valiant said.

"We'd love for one of you to tell us a bit of the history of the house on camera. Would you be willing to?" Vincent clasped his hands together.

Ramona shrugged. "I could do that, ya," she said. Valiant appreciated that—she did not want to be on camera telling horror stories.

"Great! We can do that downstairs after our session here. We're just gonna set up the night vision stuff and the EVP recorder and listen for ghostly stuff..." Vincent nodded. "Let's turn the light off again!"

Patrick nodded. "Yep, EVP ready to go."

Valiant sighed. With no vampires here, this was a lot more fun. There was no way they were going to find what they needed. The lights went out again.

"Spirits. If you're here, please talk to us," Vincent said, sitting down on the floor and turning on the EVP recorder.

"Did you hear that? It ... It sounded like... Get out?"

"I'm spooked, Pat. I think it's time to go." Vincent took a deep breath.

All of this definitely looked less spooky than the end result on YouTube, and Valiant enjoyed the show.

"Alright, let's go see what's going on outside of the attic... Oh, let's get some footage, especially of the casket..."

"This is definitely a haunted house. I think there is something here," Vincent went into narrator mode. "You can tell from the energi—"

Suddenly, there was a scream from downstairs. Valiant gasped and rushed down the ladder, throwing caution to the wind as she ran down the stairs and into a circle that had formed in the living room, leaving space in the middle. Some of the guests were running out the door. Vincent and Phil had been right behind her, Phil comedically trying to keep the camera stable as he ran.

"What happened?" She grabbed the arm of one of her guests, but they just ripped themselves loose and kept running. She briefly noticed Aubrey grabbing George and pulling her into the kitchen, and she was glad her friend would be safe, whatever was happening out there.

Then she saw. One of the grad boys was staggering, falling against the wall clutching his shoulder.
Vincent was wrestling Hannah, trying to pin her down, and a flash of metal told Valiant that the woman was holding a knife. It didn't take her long to figure out what had happened. Fed up with the advances—or perhaps after an unwanted grope—the woman had decided to show the boy what she was made of.
"I'm calling the police!" Brendon gasped, grabbing his phone and skidding over to the boy. It was a far cry from his usual, almost dancer-like grace, but right now, Valiant was just glad he wasn't running for the door as the others had.

He took off his jacket and held it against the wound.

"Ramona! Check his wound!" As a biology major, she would have a much better idea about what the damage was, and she could help Vince out.

With growing horror, Valiant saw Hannah lift the knife again, wrestling her forearm free and plunging it into Vince's arm. Immediately, the other cried out and rolled away from the exposed blade and off of Hannah.

"Oh no, you don't!" Patrick rushed over and kicked the knife out of her hand, then kicked it again to get it away from her.

"Be careful! She might have more weapons on her!" said Vincent, cradling his arm. "What the fuck did you do that for? That was just a horny teenager! Wait... have you been possessed by the ghost of Adam Lockhart?"

Valiant blinked as she realised the other seemed to care more about why she had attacked the bystander than about why she had attacked him. He had to be good, right? But then he followed up with... that. She sighed. At least a few of the frat boys were helping restrain the woman, even if she was kicking and screaming. Ramona was checking the wound, but she didn't seem too worried.

"I need you to fight this, Hannah! Don't let him take you over!" Patrick yelled.

"Hello? I need to report a stabbing. Um, address..." Brendon looked around, panicked.

"Lockhart house!" Ramona said, taking the phone and giving the address and a quick ramble of medical jargon that Valiant had no hope of understanding. At the same time, she was glad to hear her friend's voice. Between the stabbing and the ghost bullshit, it represented sanity.

Hannah had wrestled from under the boys and was getting up. Aubrey kicked her back down to the floor, a flurry of black clothes.

She felt herself run towards Hannah, grabbing her wrist and pinning it down while Patrick tried to do the same with the other arm before she could go for another weapon.

"What are we doing?" Valiant was bewildered by this turn of events. Never had she been this close to a fight, and certainly not one involving knives. She felt Hannah squirm but put her weight down.

"Well, your friend is calling the police, which is a start. You fucked up, Hannah! Fucked up!" Vincent called out, trying to stagger up. Ramona was trying to keep him down.

"Little help!" Patrick cried out. He and Valiant were struggling to keep Hannah down.

Three or so teens had not run off, so one of them helped Vincent over to the wall to sit down. The smell of blood was intense now, and Valiant ventured only a single glance back at the two. George was sniffing the air as if she was smelling the best meal of her life, and between two bleeding wounds, Valiant just hoped she could hold it together.

"I beseech the ghost of Adam Lockhart to release this woman!" Patrick bellowed.

Much to Valiant's amusement, Adam peeked out of the kitchen, making a face.

"Yes, two stab victims," said Brendon on the phone, glaring at the woman. "Yes, the perpetrator is still here."

With some joy, Valiant noticed that he described Hannah well.

Hannah gasped and pulled her arm loose from a different direction than Valiant had expected. Patrick, who hadn't gotten the best grip, to begin with, fell over as she hit him in the side of the head and then ran for the door.

The last ones to run out had left it open, but Valiant could not get herself to get up and chase the woman.

George pulled open the door to the kitchen and started chasing Hannah, running faster than Valiant had ever seen anyone in heels run. Valiant felt briefly dizzy, standing up and walking to Phil.

"Are you okay?"

"No, I'm Patrick." He grinned, then touched his temple. "I'm okay. I'm sorry I let her get away."

"Takes two to tango. I'm just glad you're not swinging a knife," Valiant said with a chuckle of relief.

A stabbing in a small town like this would immediately get everyone's full attention, which had probably been why Hannah had decided to make a break for it. Without a car and with the detailed description given, Valiant knew it wouldn't be long before she was found.

It was just a matter of time.

Chapter 31 - Valiant

It was six am. Valiant sat at the kitchen table, cleaning bone after bone of deep-fried chicken drumsticks. Now that she had given her declarations, she had been dismissed, but there was no way she could sleep.

George, Vincent, Phil, and Brendon had all given their explanations as best they could. The frat boy, she knew his name now as Scott, and Vincent had been taken to the local hospital to get themselves sorted out. Neither of them had been in critical condition, but she'd seen the relief in Ramona's eyes when actual paramedics finally saw to the wounds. It still sickened her, the violent attacks, the struggle. She briefly closed her eyes, then opened them up to count the drumsticks.

Very little made sense now. The police had placed someone outside their door to keep an eye out and ensure the woman did not return. Luckily, there were only the front door and back door, and they both had state-of-the-art locks.

George sat down across from her and slid some apple juice her way.
"You cleared those off nicely." She grinned, studying one of the drumsticks and what little had been left on it. "Thank you. For everything."

"You're damn right," Valiant said, lifting the cup of apple juice and drinking a few careful sips. She felt full and like she was going to blow up, and that was not just her overstuffed stomach. Her emotions were just as complicated right now.

"I know." She looked over. "I am very blessed with friends like you and Ramona."

"What now?" asked Valiant. "I mean. We chased her off, but what if she comes back?"

"I don't know, to be honest," said George. "I never had a problem like this. I passed on all of her details to the local Camilla Corp chapter, just in case, and I hope they can help take care of it."

"I thought you said they wouldn't help out?" Valiant frowned and grabbed a toothpick.

"Oh, if there are a few vampires in one household being threatened? That happens. But a human with possible vampire knowledge? They will track her down, especially after she hurt humans..." George sighed softly.

"Are you okay?" Valiant asked, seeing the darkness in her friend's eyes.

"I will be," George promised. "If I tell my parents, they will want me home straight away, so I'm avoiding telling them."

Ramona walked in and looked in the fridge.

"I love how those fuckers all ran, but they didn't leave a single goddamn, beer."

Brendon walked into the kitchen carrying the booze dispenser. "You hold your mouth under it, I'll open the tap. But then you must return the favour."

224

Valiant held a finger up. "Nah. Nuh-uh. Fuck that. Hang on."

She quickly got up and walked to the cupboard, taking out the punchbowl and emptying the dispenser into it.

"I cannot abide by this useless contraption, seriously," Valiant said, dumping the dispenser into the dishwasher.

"That's worries for tomorrow." She bumped it shut with her hip, then brought over some cups.

"For now, let's drink to the fact that we are all still alive."

Chapter 32

"Come on, Jack, I dare you to knock!"

"I knocked last time!" Jack huffed. "You do it!"

Tay groaned. "Laaaame." He got off of his bike.

Jack stayed at the door. At least this time, the house wasn't looking as creepy. There were three carved pumpkins outside the door, with little frilly skirts and a bunch of bows on them.

Tay took a deep breath and knocked at the door.

"Well, aren't you three a little late for trick or treating?" Adam chuckled, smiling a little. "I'm afraid we're out of candy, but we do have fried chicken."

Jack screamed, grabbed a piece of chicken from the plate, screamed again, then ran.

Tay blinked. "Uh, no thanks, I'm doing vegtober. BYE!" Both boys ran down to their bikes. Their wheels made deep marks in the soft soil as they sped off.

"It's good chicken, you guys," Jack mentioned as they drove off.

Valiant made her way to the door. "Last of the trick-or-treaters, I suppose," she laughed. She was dressed in... wait, she'd said the name. Angelic Pretty's... Magic Amulet Cutsew op! Yes. With little plastic bats in her hair, which she had teased up in a big bun. It was cute and perfectly spooky for a day like this.

"Yes. I think we can turn the lights off now." Adam crouched down and extinguished the candles in the pumpkins with a soft blow of air.

It had been a year since the YouTube incident and almost two years since the house was first disturbed. Right now, he looked as he had done in life, and he lived with the girls, a sort of caretaker. Aubrey's family had helped him gain ownership of the house with a generous donation, and the girls were living here for free when they needed the accommodation.

He walked back inside with Valiant and looked around. The girls were hosting a Halloween meet, and it was lovely to be among people.

"I still can't believe we passed all of our courses this year," Valiant sighed and sat down in one of the circles that had formed in the lounge.

Brendon had his arm around another boy and raised his drink. "Well, you managed!"

"And with honours," said George, getting up to walk over to the punchbowl to fill up her cup.

The party was definitely winding down. No, not a party. They called these get-togethers... meets. It was a lot to learn.

Aubrey looked over to Adam as he entered the kitchen. "Hey! I'm just going to, uh, get ready to stay over."

"In George's room?" He guessed, and from the blush, he knew he had hit the spot.

"Yeah..." he finally admitted.

Adam grinned. "Just as long as you behave." He shrugged. Ramona had been flirting with her girlfriend all night, and he knew that might end in a loud night. At least he had his own room these days rather than hiding in the attic.

"We're about to play Cards Against Humanity! Come join!" Ramona leaned back and peeked into the kitchen.

"Alright!" Adam called back and went to join the party.

Aubrey joined, finding a place in the circle next to George.

"Excuse me, could I just..." Petticoats ruffled and moved as Adam made a spot for himself in the circle.

A girl in a blonde ringlet wig moved over, holding on to her witch hat as she shuffled. Her name was Heather—she'd been really nice all evening. She was wearing a dark red JSK, again from that AP brand. It was called Little Witch, and he knew because most of the girls in the house had stayed up to try and secure one of the dresses from the release. Heather had gotten a lot of compliments, oohs, and aahs when she had come in in her coord. And it looked great! She had paired it with dramatic fake lashes, dark red lipstick, and a mixture of accessories ranging from a cute plastic ghost ring (again, AP, he had been told by Valiant), a bat ring from the same brand and a necklace and matching ring with an eye on it. On her lap, she had a large Usakumya[11] bag. It was a cute outfit and definitely fit the Halloween theme.

---

[11] A bag in the shape of a bear with a bunny hood on. They come in two sizes: ridiculously-small-and-fitting-a-credit-card and ridiculously-big-but-barely-fitting-anything-still.

"Alright! Who's ready to play?" Ramona called out. She was definitely a little drunk, and the girl she was dating, Amelia, put an arm around her. Kayla sighed and rolled her eyes.

"You better not do it in that dress! I'm buying it off of you one day!"

"Go suck it, Kayla. You can't afford my Twinkle Journey." Ramona stuck her tongue out. "More like tinkle journey," Ramona added. "I'ma go wee."

It was a pretty cute sight, Adam had to admit. The place felt warm, full of life. As he had meant it to be when he built it. Was his life very different from what he imagined?

Yes. But he was happy.

Flammable Penguins

Thank you for reading our little lolita adventure. It is the product of years of work from my lovely wife, with my support. We enjoy writing and making these books.

If you enjoyed it, please take a moment to let us know or leave a review. It really does make a huge difference <3

If you enjoyed this you can find her other books on FlammablePenguins.com

Vade Mecum Series
> Furcifer's Pride
> Asa's Blessing
> Kaoru's Chaos

Other Standalone Works
> Calamity at Cattori V

𝕶ickstarter 𝕵hanks

This novel would was published with the lovely support of our fans and Kickstarter backers. A huge thank you to you all, this book was for the community.

Cameo Crew

Alex
Bee Griessbach
Heather Schultz
Lara Kawa

Tea Party Pack

Carrie
Chrissii
Irma
Katie Uí Bhriain
Kerry Ashdown
Lia Solari
Paulina Pejka
Pia Salter-Ghosh
Sonia Leong

Supporters

Andie Frogley
Bethany Tomerlin Prince
Brandon Cohen
Daniela Zuckerhut
Dunning-Kruger Poster Child
Faeryndipity
Fluffy Kawaii Jo
Georgiana Mann
Ivan V.A.N. Slipper
Jack G
Jambonium
James Sharman
Karen P.
RP Wife
Saer
Tom Guida
Velvet Chocolate

Kat Inglis
Katja
Kirsty Saunders Draws
Laura Watton (PinkAppleJam)
Lisa Kruse
Louise
Megan Nowikowski
Michael S
Michyboo
Nathalie Slim
Pablo López Soriano
Raggedyman
Renee Vivian Light